LOVESWEPT IS TEN YEARS OLD, AND QUITE honestly I don't know where the time has gone. My second book, *Silver Miracles*, was one of the launch books, and I can still remember the excitement and the honor of being one of the first LOVESWEPT authors.

The int[...] [...]ely busy for me. I'[...] [...]ve been involved in [...] includ-ing the Dela[...]

One mom[...] crystallized in my memory. I had been spending long hours writing my fourth book, and one evening while I was in the kitchen, preparing dinner and talking to my youngest son, I happened to turn around and look at him, *really* look at him. That's when I suddenly realized that I was looking *up* at him. When had he grown taller than me? How could something so momentous in my child's life happen when I wasn't looking? Time. He was ecstatic. I was heartbroken.

Well, despite what I wanted—or would have permitted, had I been asked—time has passed and my two boys, Greg and Jeff, have grown up. *Fortunately* I haven't aged a bit.

Time. There's never enough of it, and it goes way too fast. If I had been put in charge of time, I would have done things a *lot* differently. Never-theless I'm looking forward to the next decade with LOVESWEPT where the only limits will be those that exist in our imagination. So, please, dear reader, join us and come along for the ride. I know we'll all have a great time.

Fayrene Preston

WHAT ARE *LOVESWEPT* ROMANCES?

They are stories of true romance and touching emotion. We believe those two very important ingredients are constants in our highly sensual and very believable stories in the LOVESWEPT line. Our goal is to give you, the reader, stories of consistently high quality that may sometimes make you laugh, sometimes make you cry, but are always fresh and creative and contain many delightful surprises within their pages.

Most romance fans read an enormous number of books. Those they truly love, they keep. Others may be traded with friends and soon forgotten. We hope that each LOVESWEPT romance will be a treasure—a "keeper." We will always try to publish

LOVE STORIES YOU'LL NEVER FORGET
BY AUTHORS YOU'LL ALWAYS REMEMBER

The Editors

Loveswept ® 620

WHAT EMILY WANTS

FAYRENE PRESTON

BANTAM BOOKS

NEW YORK • TORONTO • LONDON • SYDNEY • AUCKLAND

ONE

Emily Stanton strolled along the upstairs gallery that overlooked the reception hall of the elegant North Dallas mansion, idly trailing her fingers atop the marble balustrade. From her position above the hall she had a spectacular view of the gala party taking place.

Deliberately separating herself from the throng below, she had thought the height would give her a truer perspective. But the party looked the same as it had when she had been in its midst. Beautiful gowns whirled and swayed and shone with expensive luster, jewels flashed and sparkled and dazzled, women sought and beckoned, men jockeyed for information and position.

It was a power party, and the center of its power was Jay Barrett.

It was his house, his party, and the people here were his guests. He stood at one end of the hall, where men and women alike manuevered to be near him, seeking his attention and favor.

From her position Emily could see him clearly, his dark-blond head bending to catch what a coquettish woman next to him was saying. Though she couldn't see the color of his eyes from this distance, she knew from previous encounters that it was a deep, leaf green, undiluted by striations of any other color.

His eyes fascinated her. Their expression told her they were accustomed to lies, and because of it she found it difficult to tell him anything other than the truth, whether she wanted to or not.

His powerful, compelling face was made up of sharp contours and deeply grooved lines and gave her the impression that the person living behind the face had fought many battles and along the way had experienced darkness and suffering. Much as she would like to, she couldn't dismiss the fact that somehow she knew he had clawed and scratched his way through life, and despite tremendous odds, had endured. Oh, his face didn't actually bear scars, but the lack of physical evidence didn't matter. She knew. . . .

And the knowledge made it hard for her to turn away from him . . . because, quite simply, he looked on the outside like she felt on the inside. *Scarred and battered.*

But in his case he had also triumphed.

She knew nothing about triumph.

"Champagne, miss?"

Emily turned to see a white-gloved waiter bearing a silver tray. She took one of the crystal glasses and sipped its pale, sparkling contents. The bubbles tickled her throat and warmed her insides in an unfamiliar way, just as the silk fabric of the gown she wore felt unfamiliar against her skin.

Jay had paid for the champagne, and he had also paid for the silk-and-flocked-velvet gown she wore. He had said the gold creation was a gift for her to keep. But she wouldn't. In her life there was no place for silk-and-flocked-velvet gowns.

The woman now standing beside him had golden-blond hair and an ivory-tinted bosom that appeared in imminent jeopardy of bursting free from her low-necked gown. And she was looking at Jay as if he were a piece of dark, rich chocolate she would love to consume but wasn't sure she dared.

She had noticed that the vast majority of the women present tonight looked at him in the same way. The men on the other hand responded to him with deference and respect. Some even tried to treat him in a casual, familiar way.

He was pleasant and cordial to all, but from what she could see, he gave none his friendship.

She looked back at the woman who had laid a tentative hand on his arm. Foolish, foolish woman. Didn't she know she was no match for someone who could walk through fire and emerge on the other side whole and even stronger?

Just then Jay's gaze swung upward and pinned her with its piercing intensity. He had known where she was all the time, she realized without surprise. He made a slight movement of his head, and she knew that he wanted her to come to him.

He was too formidable to play games with, too inherently dangerous to anger, but she stayed where she was.

She had to keep her guard up with him at all times. Not that that would be difficult. When had she ever lived any other way?

As the last of his guests departed, Jay turned to his butler. "Everything went very well, John. Thank you, and be sure to give my thanks to Roberta." Roberta was John's wife, and together the two of them ran Jay's house.

John nodded. "I'll do that. She'll be pleased. Will there be anything else, sir?"

John's formality secretly amused Jay, but he had learned to keep it to himself. When John had first come to work for him, he had told him there was no need for such rigid formality, but the man persisted. Roberta, on the other hand, was an entirely different matter. "No. I'll see you in the morning."

Jay pulled his tie loose from its knot as he made his way down the hall to his study. Inside the book-lined, paneled room, the light from two lamps was

producing a pale, intimate glow. Two deeply cush-
ioned wing-backed chairs faced each other in front
of the fireplace, where, even though outside it was a
warm, late-spring night, a fire burned.

Without pausing to speak to the occupant of one of
the chairs, he strode to the wall behind his desk where
an oil painting depicting long-horned cattle grazing on
scrub-dotted land hung. He had always admired the
breed for their ability to endure despite great odds, so
he had specially commissioned the painting.

With a flick of a hidden latch the painting swung
away from the wall to reveal a safe. Moments later he
withdrew a slim bundle of bills bound by a wide rubber
band. With money in hand, he closed the safe, repositioned the picture, and crossed to Emily.

As he dropped down into the chair opposite her, he
tossed the bundle of bills into her lap.

She looked down at the money, but she didn't touch
it.

What was she thinking? he wondered. Two weeks
ago he had for the first time walked into the florist shop
where she worked and seen her fresh flower arrangements on display. He had been struck by the wild beauty of the arrangements. They had fairly burst with lif
and passion.

Then he had seen her—exquisitely lovely, frustra
ingly quiet and reserved.

In the time since, he had actively pursued her, an
each time he saw her, it was like seeing her for the

first time all over again. He always found something new over which to marvel. Tonight it was the way the lamplight brought out the rich golden tones of her brown hair until it appeared the color of dark honey. In fact he had chosen the gold gown for her to wear this evening because of her hair, the amber color of her eyes, and the golden undertone of her ivory skin.

But what was she thinking?

True, it was her beauty that had first attracted him to her. But what had kept him coming back, what had continued to intrigue him much more than her beauty, were the contradictions he sensed within her.

Her eyes held true innocence and at the same time a deep knowledge of sin. And the fusion of the two elements touched a chord somewhere deep inside him. He had grown almost single-minded in his need to taste of her innocence and to plumb the mysterious depths of her sin.

And the contradictions didn't end there.

Sitting across from him now, all ivory and gold, she appeared the embodiment of strength and dignity. Yet he would swear he had never seen anyone look so frag-ile, so extremely breakable.

What was the truth? What was the lie?

She stared down at the bundle for a moment longer, then lifted her head and gazed at him. "Do you want to know what my first impression of you was?"

He smiled faintly. "Something tells me I should say

no, but in this case I'll waive my good judgment. Go ahead."

"I thought you were insufferably presumptuous and arrogant."

"When you *do* speak, you don't mince words, do you?" His smile broadened. "I don't suppose anything has happened to change your mind about me in the last two weeks?"

"Nothing."

"Yet you're here."

"For the moment."

He tensed, but with the next heartbeat he forced himself to relax. Even if he had to move heaven and earth, he would somehow find a way to get to know her better, to have her get to know him. And to flat out have her in every possible way. He wouldn't allow her to get away from him. Not yet. He casually undid the top three buttons of his shirt. "I thought you were going to stay."

She glanced again at the money in her lap. She needed it and the rest of the money he had promised her with a desperation that had her mouth dry. She had been frantic with worry over money for so long that she had forgotten what it was like *not* to worry about it. And even though the amount he offered wouldn't be a permanent solution to her problem, it would certainly provide relief for the immediate future.

In theory the deal he had offered her sounded wonderful, but the reality was an entirely different matter.

She just had to decide whether or not the price she would have to pay for the money would be too high. "I don't know."

"I've been up front with you, Emily."

His statement almost made her smile, but smiling wasn't something she did easily. "No one could ever accuse you of beating around the bush," she said dryly. "You walked into the shop, took one look at me, and said, 'I want you to arrange the flowers for my party. And I want you.' "

"And you said, 'It will cost you extra—for the flowers.' "

The statement had amazed her as much as it had amazed him, and she still wasn't sure why she had said it. It had been totally out of character for her. Long ago she had learned to stifle any smart-aleck remark or even a quick retort that could be misunderstood. But the words had come out of her mouth before they had reached her consciousness, and she could find no explanation for them. "I suppose I thought outrageousness would be the best way to handle outrageousness."

"Refreshingly honest is more like it. As a matter of fact I don't think anyone has ever gotten my attention as fast as you did."

"I didn't want your attention."

"Didn't you?"

She fought against the urge to squirm beneath his probing gaze. She hadn't lied, yet he had a way of making her mentally double-check herself. "No."

"Well, no matter. Whatever your intention, you got it. I was quite taken with you." More truthfully he had become obsessed, he thought wryly, and now that he had gotten her this far, he wasn't going to risk her bolting by revealing the full extent of his interest. "Most people aren't honest about what they want. I admire those who are. I admire you."

"It was just a flip remark."

"Is that really all it was?"

This time she couldn't stop herself from shifting uneasily, and the silk of the dress slid against her skin. Suddenly the gown seemed as if it were too tight, constricting her upper body, preventing her from drawing a deep breath. Yet the dress fit her perfectly.

"I *never* in a million years expected you to offer me money," she said, her voice rising a fraction. "People just don't do things like that."

"As a matter of fact, Emily, they do."

"Then you live in a different world than I do."

"We live in the same world. Up to now we've simply been inhabiting different places in that world. But I've been where you are now, wanting, needing. . . ."

Irritated, she shook her head. "I don't believe in psychoanalysis, Jay, and I hate it when people try to figure me out."

He held up a hand, a sign of conciliation. "All right, we all have secrets—"

"I *don't* have secrets.

"And it was just a moment ago that I was commenting on your honesty," he said, his tone gently chiding. If she grew any more still, he thought, she would turn to stone. "So, Emily, what are we going to do? Try as you might, I don't think we can get away from the fact that I have offered you money in return for your company, and you agreed."

Panic seized her, and nausea rose in her throat. When he had first brought up the idea of paying her for ten days of her time and had named an amount, she had been too stunned to say anything. Then to her further consternation and astonishment, he had taken her silence for a bargaining tactic and had proceeded to raise the amount higher and higher until finally, in alarm, she had yelled for him to stop.

And then she had agreed.

"I remember," she said, giving no sign of the fight she was having to maintain her inner composure.

He nodded toward her lap. "Five thousand dollars in ten five-hundred-dollar bills." He paused. "You know, Emily, most people use electronic banking these days, especially when it comes to an amount of that size, or at the very least a cashier's check."

"I wanted to see it."

He understood completely. "Because you don't trust anything you can't see."

"Why should I?"

Why should she indeed? Oh, yes. Whether she knew it or not, he did understand. If he could only get her to let her guard down, she would see they had a great deal in common.

But she remained maddeningly enigmatic, with that intriguing quality of stillness to her. Another contradiction. Even when she had been strolling along the second-floor gallery earlier this evening, she had appeared still, as if she kept everything that was important about her and to her inside herself, where she protected it. He wanted to see inside her, he wanted to *be* inside her. Sweet hell, he did. "You look beautiful tonight," he said huskily. "Did I tell you?"

"Yes."

She had spent all day at the shop, arranging the flowers for his party. Then while Harriet—her boss and the owner of the shop—and several delivery people had delivered the flowers, she had rushed home, taken a quick shower, and driven to his house.

She had been directed upstairs to a large blue-and-gold bedroom, where she had found the dress and shoes on the bed. She had never seen a dress so lovely, never worn a dress so obviously expensive. She had almost left then, but her financial need was critical, and in the end she had put on the dress and shoes and descended the stairs to Jay. That was when he had told her how beautiful she was, and to her dismay her pulse had raced out of control at the compliment.

"Did you have a good time at the party?" he asked, watching her closely.

"Does it matter? I attended the party as you directed."

"You sound as if I gave you an order. It was only a request. Being able to see you made the party more bearable for me."

"More bearable? Why give a party if you don't want to be there?"

"The party served several purposes, not the least of which is goodwill in the community. Besides, it wasn't too bad—even if you wouldn't stay beside me."

She shrugged uncomfortably. "Staying beside you wasn't part of the deal."

"You're absolutely right. I asked only that you come to the party—that, and move in here with me for ten days."

Only. She stood, and the money fell from her lap to the floor, but she was so busy struggling with a question, she barely noticed.

And the question persisted: *Could one move into a tiger's lair and remain whole?*

"You've complied with the first part of the deal," he said quietly. "Do you intend to comply with the rest of it?"

Besieged by thoughts and feelings she couldn't adequately define, she was unable to think clearly. "I don't know."

The change in his expression was almost imperceptible, but there was no mistaking the implacable steel that entered his voice.

"We had an agreement, Emily, and I expect you to honor that agreement. And because I do, I have nine more packets of money in the safe just like the one in your lap."

"You have forty-five thousand dollars in cash in your safe?" She couldn't keep her astonishment from her voice.

"That's the amount we agreed upon."

There was no getting around it—she had agreed. But it had been more out of shock than accord.

"Do you want more?" he asked, his gaze intent. "Is that it? Go ahead. Name your price."

She felt the color leach from her skin. "You're crazy."

"About you," he agreed, his face hard. "Raise the ante, Emily. I'll meet it."

"*No.* Good heavens, don't you see? I'm not sure I can take the amount you're offering."

He eyed her curiously. "You don't want more?"

She would love more, but the idea of taking *any* amount from him was already making her sick to her stomach. "How could I?" She gestured to the floor. "That's a *huge* amount."

"Don't worry about it," he said curtly. "I can afford it."

"That doesn't make me feel any better."

"Then what *would*? Tell me and I'll do it. Or say it. Or anything else it takes. You're in an amazing position, Emily. There are scores of people who would back me up on this. I'm willing to do just about anything you say, give you anything. All you have to do is reach out and take it—and stay with me."

She wrapped her arms around her waist. "I don't know," she whispered.

"Emily, you *agreed*."

"I agreed so that you would stop calling me at work, stop coming by, and stop sending all those gifts."

"Which you sent back."

"I had to. I didn't know you. I *don't* know you."

He smiled with satisfaction. "Exactly. That's why you're here. You wouldn't accept any of my offers to go out, and this is the only way I could think of to get to spend any time with you."

"By *paying* me?"

"If I had arranged for us to be flown to Paris for dinner in my jet as I wanted to, it would have cost me much more."

The idea was so foreign to her, she couldn't help but ask, "Do you do this sort of thing often? Pay a woman for her time?"

"No, Emily, in that respect you're absolutely unique."

Once again nausea rose in her throat. She pressed a hand to her mouth, fighting the sick feeling, all the while telling herself that there was no need to be upset. It was a business-type arrangement, nothing more.

He stood and stretched down to pick up the money. When he straightened, he gazed thoughtfully at her. "I can see where you might be wary of moving in with a complete stranger, but if you don't know me personally, you must at least be aware of my reputation."

Who wasn't? she wondered ruefully. He was well known in the Dallas business community and also in the city's society circles. He had been a longtime patron of another florist shop before its owners had decided to retire. They had referred him to Harriet, and she still remembered how excited Harriet had been at the prospect of having his business.

"You'll be safe with me, Emily. If I threaten to turn out to be some kind of pervert, you can always pick up the phone and call the newspaper. With one phone call you could ruin my reputation forever in this town." For the moment he decided not to tell her that he could care less what the newspapers printed about him.

She had never even considered that he might be someone who would do her physical harm, and she was somewhat surprised that she hadn't. But looking back, she supposed that right from the beginning she had instinctively known he would never need to use physical force. He could have whatever he wanted from most women just by crooking his finger.

"For a solid two weeks you refused every invitation I made you, so it's depressingly easy for me to conclude that you're not interested in me.

"You're right, I'm not." He could have whatever he wanted from most women, but not from her. The whole idea of succumbing to his charms frightened her. She would never give herself to any man.

"No, of course you're not," he murmured in a dry tone. "That being the case, I'll immediately leap to another conclusion and guess that you must have some other reason for considering my offer." The longer she remained silent, the more tense he became. "So," he prodded, "would you tell me what the other reason is?"

"No."

He tapped one end of the packet against his fingertips. "Whatever the reason, it must be something pretty important."

Her head jerked, sending her hair flying behind her shoulders. "What difference does it make? Maybe I want to go on a round-the-world trip. Maybe I want to buy fifty thousand dollars' worth of jewelry. Maybe I want to give it all to charity. Whatever my reason, it's not any of your business, and it's certainly not something I want to discuss."

"Okay. You don't have to tell me the reason why you're doing this—you . . . just . . . have . . . to . . . do . . . it."

She moved, walking the perimeter of the room. He watched her as she studied the art he had collected over the years and the leather-bound books he sometimes read deep into the night. He watched her, taking in her aloofness and her beauty. And his need for her grew.

She stopped at his prize Monet. Tilting her head,

she examined the flowered landscape that looked as if the artist had seen the garden through a soft mist. Then she glanced over at his painting of the longhorns that hung behind his desk. He didn't have to be a mind reader to know that she was wondering why he had two such different paintings in the same room.

If she asked him, he would tell her, but she didn't. She moved on, finally stopping in front of his desk.

"Is fifty thousand dollars really so little to you?" she asked, staring down at the large onyx-and-gold pen set resting squarely in the center of the desk's highly polished surface.

"An amount of money, *any* amount, is relative, Emily. The point is, I'm used to paying for what I want. In my experience all women want something, it's just a question of what."

She drew the pen from its sheath, released it so that it fell back into place, then repeated the action. "It sounds as if you haven't had very good experiences with women."

"Let's just say my theory hasn't been proven wrong."

Color crept up her skin. *She* certainly hadn't proved his theory wrong, she thought, inexplicably annoyed.

"You don't fall into that category, Emily," he said softly. "You're much more honest than most."

Then why didn't she feel honest? she wondered, releasing the pen for the final time.

"And anyway, I'm actually more comfortable with paying for something than I am with receiving something as a gift. Apparently you feel the same way since you wouldn't accept any of my gifts."

She turned around and looked at him. "I've already told you why I didn't, but there's also another reason. I didn't accept them because I knew your gifts came with price tags."

He walked to her and casually brushed a shining length of her hair behind her bare shoulders. It wasn't the first time he had touched her. In fact touching her had become almost a compulsion with him.

In the beginning he had kept his touch light and casual so as not to startle her. Despite his care, she had been startled anyway, but after the first few times she seemed to have grown used to his hands on her hair and on her skin. He drew great satisfaction from that knowledge. "You were absolutely right to think that," he said quietly. "But you can relax. I'm not giving you a gift now. You will be earning the money."

Maybe the concept of earning such a tremendous amount of money was the problem, she thought. She was used to working hard for an hourly wage, but fifty thousand dollars . . . "I can't even begin to imagine what I can do to earn that much money."

"It's a matter of supply and demand, Emily. I want your company, and the past two weeks have shown me that it's in damned short supply. To be even more precise, it's completely unavailable to me. Therefore your company is worth a great deal to me."

Another problem identified. "My company," she

repeated dully. "If we told ten people what we were about to do, nine out of ten of those people would call me a prostitute."

"Then they would be wrong, wouldn't they?"

He skimmed his hand over her hair. His touch was so gentle, his voice so quiet, his gaze so mesmerizing.

"Leave other people out of this, Emily. This is between you and me, and we'll make up our own rules."

"Is that really possible?" Her tone was almost wistful.

"I've done it my whole life."

"I've never been able to."

"Take the money, and you'll be able to." He held out the packet. "Take it, Emily. And every night for the next nine nights I'll give you another bundle just like this one. It's the method of payment you requested. See? Already I'm abiding by one of your rules."

She had made the stipulation because she hadn't trusted that he would give her the total amount at the end of the ten days. She looked at the money, but crossed her arms in front of herself.

He made it sound so easy—why was she hesitating? Realistically she knew there was simply no way he would ever get his money's worth. But having a conscience was a luxury she couldn't afford, just as feeling cheap was. He was offering her an answer to a situation she had thought hopeless. She was absolutely crazy not to snap it up before he changed his mind. And she would.

But . . . "Tell me again what our time together would entail."

He withdrew his extended hand and the money. "Basically just that, time spent together. If you like, you can consider yourself my resident flower arranger. After all, that's what you said, 'The flowers will cost you extra.' "

But, she thought, he had also said, "I want you."

"Were you able to take off the next two weeks from work?"

She had worked for Harriet only nine months and wasn't entitled to vacation time. But Harriet liked both her and her work, and when she had told her she needed the time for personal reasons, Harriet had agreed. As for her part-time waitress job, which Jay didn't know about, she would have to quit and simply hope to get a similar job at some other place. "Not two weeks, Jay. Ten days. Remember? You said ten days."

"No, *you* said ten days. If I'd had my way, I would have asked for ten months or maybe even ten years." He slid his hand over her shoulder, then back again. "So? Did you get the time off?"

Heat shivered through her at his touch. Ignore it, she told herself once again, just as she had each time in the last two weeks he had reached out to her. His touch was always casual, always gentle, never threatening. She had decided she had to be imagining its ability to invade the depths of her body. "If I want time off, I can take it. But . . ."

An eyebrow cocked. "But?"

"I know I brought this up before, but I want to be absolutely sure . . ."

He knew what was coming. "About what?"

"You don't expect me to sleep with you, do you?"

He slowly smiled. "No, Emily. I don't expect it. I want you to—I've already told you so—but no, I don't expect it."

She fixed him with a direct gaze. "There will be *no* sex, Jay. I might let you pay me to be with you, to arrange your flowers, but I won't, I *can't*, let you pay me for sex."

He curved his hand along her jawline to ensure that she wouldn't look away. "And I don't want to pay you for sex. Making love with you is something I want for free."

His low, husky voice made her nerves tingle, and she could feel her skin burning beneath his palm. She tried to swallow and couldn't. Her mouth had been dry before, but now her whole body felt positively parched. "There is nothing free in life."

He bent so that his gaze was even with hers. "I know that better than most, and to tell the truth, I want you so badly, I would probably take you any way I could get you. But here's another truth: When you come to my bed, I want you to come because you want to be there more than you want to breathe, and *not* for money."

She had thought his eyes a solid green, but now she saw glimmering flecks the color of fire surrounding the pupil. She had viewed him as dangerous. Now she knew that if she allowed it, he could be fatal.

She cleared her throat and lifted her hand to push his away from her face. "Understand me, Jay. You can't have me, and you can't buy me. Somehow, some way, you and I seem to have entered into what is a preposterous agreement. But I'm giving you a portion of my time, nothing else."

"Then you're going to stay?"

She was afraid. Deep-down, icy-cold, gut-clenchingly afraid. Of exactly what, though, she didn't know. But then again it didn't really matter what it was.

She might be scared, she might be apprehensive, she might be crazy to even consider saying yes, but when all was said and done, there was one clear, shining truth staring her straight in the face: *In this matter she had no choice.*

"All right. Yes."

He extended his hand to her once more, and this time she took the money.

"Good," he said, his voice blatant with satisfaction. "I'm glad it's settled. Now, we should talk about where you're going to put the money. First of all, I hope you'll agree that it's not safe to carry so much around. But if you try to deposit five thousand dollars in cash every day, or even two or three times a week, I guarantee you that the bank teller will notify the police. They'll want to know where it came from."

She put a hand to her head. Lord, she hadn't even considered that cash would be a problem.

"If you like, I can arrange for my bank—"

"I'll make my own arrangements," she said tightly.

"All right, then on to the next question. Do you like the bedroom where you changed earlier this evening, because if you don't—"

"It's fine," she said, then a thought occurred. "How close is it to yours?"

He smiled. "You'll only be a few feet away from me. My bedroom is behind the double doors at the end of the hall."

"Maybe another room would be better for me."

"Sorry, you've already said that bedroom would be fine. Did you bring your things with you?"

"No. I wasn't sure I'd stay." But she had been. Any other thought or hesitation had been a denial of reality. "I won't need much. I'll go home and pack a few things."

"I'll drive you tomorrow."

"No." It was an instantaneous, gut reaction. She didn't want him to see where she lived, didn't want him to be able to find her after these ten days were over. Then she remembered he knew where she worked. She lifted her chin. "Just because you're paying me doesn't mean we have to be together every waking hour."

"Actually it does. But we'll see. . . . Who knows, maybe I'll grow tired of you."

She felt a disconcerting pang and chose to think of

it as panic concerning the money. "If that happens, does that mean I won't get the entire fifty thousand?"

"One day at a time, remember? That's what you said. Five thousand dollars for one day and one night."

It was now clear to her that she had said too much. "It's late. Since I didn't bring any of my things, I'll go home for tonight, but I'll be back in the morning."

He shook his head. "No, Emily. The money you just accepted includes tonight. And I'm being generous. You haven't given me a full day of your time yet."

"But—"

"You'll find some things up in the room in the closet and in the bureau. I bought them when I bought your dress. Everything you need is there."

There it was—a sterling example of why she had hesitated. She had a basic, genuine concern that he would overwhelm her, that he would take her over, and strangely, that ultimately he might possibly destroy her.

Jay Barrett was unlike anyone she had ever had to deal with. He was a force that respected no barriers, no obstacles. He was a man who, from what she had seen, always got what he wanted. And he had said he wanted her in his bed.

But she needed to remember that, in this case, her concern was irrational. He might touch her with his gentle hands, his dark, piercing gazes, and his soft, hot words, but she would be safe. He would never touch her heart.

The past had ensured that her heart was invulnerable.

"Then I'd like to go to my room now. I'm tired."

He nodded. "If you need me, press *One* on the bedside phone, and I'll answer."

"I won't need anything." And she especially wouldn't need *him*, she thought to herself. The possibility didn't exist.

"In that case I'll see you in the morning."

She walked slowly to the door, expecting at any moment that he would stop her with a touch, a word, or even a look. But when she reached the door without any of those things happening, she didn't immediately take the escape it offered. Instead she paused and looked back.

His brows rose. "Yes?"

"Have you ever taken a woman to Paris for dinner?"

"No," he said, his voice a husky caress, "but you I would have."

TWO

Emily awoke at dawn. Lying in the big bed, she listened for any sounds that might indicate someone else in the house was awake. She couldn't hear anything, and she wasn't surprised. The house was so big, there could be a convention going on in another part and she wouldn't hear it.

She sat up in the bed and surveyed the room. The finely woven sheets on which she had slept were the color of a clear, blue sky. The same blue color—but this time with gold flecks woven through the material—made up the canopy over her head and matched the feather comforter at her feet. Across the expanse of thick white carpet there was a dressing table with a large gilt-edged mirror above it. Crystal bottles filled with sweet-smelling lotions and perfumes covered the top of the dressing table. Yards and yards of blue-and-gold taffeta were swagged and bunched at the windows.

Two overstuffed chairs were placed by the window, a table between them. A silver tray bearing a crystal and silver decanter of water and an exquisite goblet graced the table.

For the first time in her life she was surrounded by luxury, but under the circumstances she couldn't enjoy it.

Her nerves were wound tight, too tight, and she didn't have to ask herself why. She had agreed to participate in a highly unusual arrangement. But feeling temporarily off balance was the least of her worries.

She was about to spend a great deal of time with Jay Barrett, a powerful man in terms of money, influence, and personal charisma.

She wasn't worried about his money or even his influence. He was paying for her time only because she was allowing him to. She had settled that fact in her mind last night. And her normal, everyday life didn't fall within the circle of his influence. True, he was now a patron of the florist shop where she worked, and Harriet was overjoyed. If it came down to it, Harriet just might choose Jay's patronage over her job. But if that happened, she would simply get another job. She had changed jobs before, and she would do it again if she had to. In the meantime she refused to worry about what would happen nine days from now.

His charisma . . .

The man fairly radiated a sexuality that seemed to have a way of building on itself until at times he almost burned with it. More than once last night her heart had raced merely at his closeness.

His touch combined sensuality with a gentleness and an experienced sureness that a couple of times had come close to undoing her. She made a sound of frustration.

It didn't matter. Nothing mattered except the money.

It would no doubt surprise Jay to know that she was a virgin. In his circle virgins were probably as rare as unicorns. In this day and time women simply didn't reach the age of twenty-six with their virginity intact. But she had. And it had been easy.

More than one man had accused her of being made of ice, but she had been unable to sympathize with them. Not only had she not had any desire to become involved with anyone, she had been too busy earning a living and more recently taking care of her mother. Which brought her to the main reason why she was finding it hard to enjoy her surroundings.

She couldn't in good conscience enjoy living amid such luxury when her mother lay in a nursing home that featured tasteless meals, filth, and stench.

Though Jay had had no way of knowing, his timing had been perfect. On the day he had offered her his so-called deal, she had just come from visiting her mother. She had found her lying in a soiled bed that hadn't been changed for hours, and her wrists had been tied to the bed with rags. And it wasn't the first time she had found her restrained and filthy.

While she was with her mother, she had controlled her tears. She had changed the bed herself, bathed her mother, and fed her breakfast, going slowly, making sure her mother got enough to eat. But when she had left, she had broken down into tears of frustration and grief.

Money. It had been a problem for as long as she could remember. While she had been in high school, she had worked part-time as a waitress, saving as much as she could. As soon as she graduated, she had moved out of the house and gone to work full-time. But she had stayed close by, keeping in touch with her mother, fearing that the day would come when her mother would need her. And it had.

Through no fault of her own, her mother had been partially, but apparently permanently paralyzed in a senseless, violent act. And along with the paralysis had come other health problems that had virtually made her an invalid. It wasn't fair that she should have to live out the rest of her life in such bleak, depressing surroundings, receiving inferior medical treatment and being taken care of by an overworked and underpaid staff.

The medical insurance had been quickly depleted even before they had left Houston. Circumstances and government cutbacks made aid impossible. Since she had been in Dallas, she had put in long hours every day at her job at the florist shop, plus waiting on tables Saturday night and Sunday. But with all her hard work and careful saving, the nursing home was the only one she could afford, and she hadn't known how she was going to handle her mother's next medical emergency.

Until Jay had made his offer.

She reached beneath the pillow and pulled out the money. Five thousand dollars. It was enough to put her mother in a decent place and keep her there for two months, maybe a little longer. She had had one in mind for months. It wasn't anything fancy, but it was neat and clean and surprisingly cheerful, and the personnel who worked there were conscientious. The other forty-five thousand would add an additional eighteen to twenty months, with competent help and medical care, and as a very large bonus, physical therapy, something her mother desperately needed.

And during that time she could work even harder and save so that when Jay's money was gone . . .

She sighed. She'd figure something out when the time came. She'd have to. But for now she *had* to get her mother out of the place she was in.

She slipped from the bed and went to shower. Minutes later, dressed in her own cotton skirt and blouse that she had worn to the house yesterday, she was quietly descending the stairs.

"Good morning."

She started and looked over the side of the railing. Jay stood there, in slacks and a sports shirt, holding a cup of coffee.

For a moment he saw it, her innocence exposed and

unguarded, like that of a startled fawn caught in the bright glare of the oncoming headlights of a truck. In her mind, he assumed, he represented the truck, the danger. He just wished he knew why. In the next moment the innocence quickly vanished, to be replaced by the jaded acceptance of someone with a firsthand knowledge of sin.

His life hadn't been easy, and he had overcome many an obstacle to get where he was today, but at the moment he couldn't ever remember facing a more daunting, more interesting challenge than Emily.

"Going somewhere?" His tone was politely interested.

She continued down the stairs until she reached the entry hall, where he joined her. "I was going home. I thought I could get there, pack my things, and be back before you woke up."

"I've been up for a couple of hours."

"Why?" If she'd given the matter any thought at all, she imagined she would have believed that anyone as rich as Jay would sleep late.

"I'm usually up this early. Today I've been trying to get some work out of the way so that I can take the day off." Her face was scrubbed free of any makeup this morning, and he couldn't resist reaching out to lightly run his fingertips across the velvet skin of her cheek.

Emily felt his touch with mixed emotions. It was as if he had some fetish concerning her skin, and she didn't understand his compulsion, or for that matter her reaction.

In her life she had rarely been touched, and contrary to what the experts said about human beings needing to be touched, she had never missed it. In fact she had been grateful.

But then Jay had come along. Now she was not only used to the feel of his hand gliding over her, her skin seemed to drink it in greedily. But her reaction wasn't anything to become overwrought about. It wasn't as if he were doing something as intimate as caressing her breasts . . . or taking one of her nipples into his mouth. . . .

Her breasts began to swell, and her nipples tightened and began to throb.

She cleared her throat and attempted to focus on him. "You *own* the company. You can take off anytime you like."

He dropped his hand back to his side. "That's true, but if I want the company to be there when I get back, I have to make sure that all bases are covered before I leave." He paused. "Did you sleep well?"

"Yes." The evening had left her exhausted, or to be more precise, dealing with Jay had. Despite her unfamiliar surroundings she had fallen fast asleep.

"And what about the nightgown and robe I bought for you? Did they fit?"

By no stretch of the imagination could the negligee set she found when she had gone upstairs be called a nightgown and robe. It was a diaphanous bit of lace and sheer nothing that must have cost the earth, and she had been too unnerved by its inherent sensuality to sleep in it. "I don't know. I didn't wear either piece."

"Then you slept naked." His voice lowered to a growl. "If I had known that, I wouldn't have been able to sleep at all." As it was, thoughts of her being so close had filled his mind, and sleep had come only after hours of tossing and turning.

Desire sounded in his voice, but she refused to be concerned about the sexual awareness he could conjure in her so effortlessly. With everything else she had to contend with, she would go mad if she did.

"I can understand why you thought I would need a dress to wear to your party. My wardrobe obviously doesn't run to that sort of thing. But why on earth would you buy me something like that negligee set?"

He shrugged. "I saw it and immediately thought of how beautiful you would look in it."

The idea of him imagining her wearing the negligee set had her nerves scraping against one another. "You shouldn't be thinking things like that." She nearly flinched, because even to her ears her words sounded defensive and prudish. She could only imagine what he thought.

His eyes darkened. "Every time I look at you, Emily, I want to take you right then and there, no matter where we happen to be or who's around us. Now, I'm managing—just barely—to control those urges, but there is no way I can control the things that go on in my mind."

Her senses went crazy. "I see," she said slowly, giving her equilibrium a chance to even. It was a given that he was going to say outrageous things. She simply had to learn not to react. "So what you're saying is that I shouldn't complain."

"Complain all you want, but you've got nothing to worry about from me. Do you believe me?"

"I'm trying."

"I told you—not until you want me more than you want to breathe."

"It's not going to happen, Jay. I like breathing a lot."

"I didn't say you'd have to stop." With a casual movement he glanced at his watch. "Why don't we go have breakfast, and then I'll take you home to pack."

Her instinct was to argue that she wanted to go home by herself, but she quickly decided that it wouldn't be worth the effort. She'd let him have this round because, quite simply, it wasn't important. There was nothing at her apartment of importance to her and therefore nothing she minded him seeing.

What *was* important was to keep this time with him in proper perspective. The amount of money he was paying her would allow her to make her mother's life better. And for that she would do just about *anything*—anything, that is, that didn't involve her heart.

*   *   *

"Your car stands out like a sore thumb in this neighborhood," Emily said, worriedly gazing out the front window of her small duplex apartment at Jay's Mercedes-Benz, which was parked curbside. "And your wax job is on its way to being ruined. The neighborhood kids are getting their fingerprints all over it."

"Fingerprints won't stop it from running," he said. "However, if they start taking apart the motor, let me know."

He sounded so unconcerned, she turned and looked at him. His presence was so powerful, his six-foot plus frame seemed to be taking up most of the space in the front room. "You don't care that they're all over it?"

"Why should I? They're just curious."

She remembered all the pickup trucks her step-father, Ralph, had owned over the years. Washing and waxing it had been a weekend ritual with him when she had been growing up, and he hadn't been able to tolerate even the smallest smudge.

"Who's this?" Jay asked, picking up a framed photograph of a young woman smiling radiantly down at the baby she was holding in her arms.

She had forgotten the photograph. It was of her mother when she had been young and happy, and the picture was very precious to her. The sight of Jay holding it made her anxious. If he got mad and threw it or even if he dropped it. . . .

She stopped herself and waited until she could speak without betraying the inner tremor her thoughts had caused her. "That's my mother and me," she said evenly. "I was only about six weeks old there." Why, she wondered belatedly, hadn't she simply told him it was a picture of an aunt and a cousin, or someone else equally unimportant? The less he knew about her, the easier it would be for her to keep a distance between them.

"She's lovely," he said, replacing the photograph on a battered oak side table. "You look like her."

"I know."

"Does she live nearby?"

Emily hesitated. "Yes."

"What about your father? Do they still live together?"

Again she hesitated. "My father died when I was only a baby."

He gazed thoughtfully at her for a long moment, then glanced around the room, frowning. "How long have you lived here?"

She was beginning to feel as if she were on a witness stand, and she didn't like it. "Not long. Less than a year." She, too, looked at the room, wondering what it was that was bothering him. But she didn't see anything remarkable. There was a sofa and two chairs, all three average-looking, all three a worn brown-and-white tweed. Placed in front of the sofa and between the two chairs were occasional tables made of laminated plastic laid over pressed wood. Everything in the house belonged to her landlord. The apartment was functional and cheap, and that's all she cared about.

"You've lived here almost a year?" His tone held more than a touch of curiosity.

"Actually I said *less* than a year." She looked around again and saw a neat, clean room. She gave up trying to guess what was bothering him. "What is your fascination with this room?"

"It's just so bare and impersonal. With the exception of your mother's picture, there's nothing of you here."

She clenched her teeth. "What is so amazing about that? I don't have money to waste on decorating. Besides, what difference does it make? I'm hardly ever here, and when I am, I sleep."

He rocked back on his heels. "So what you're saying is that your home isn't important to you."

She'd had enough of the subject. "Look, why don't you sit down, and I'll go into the bedroom and pack my things. It won't take me long."

"Can I help in any way?"

"Why on *earth* would I need help?" She closed her eyes and sighed. Her nerves were showing. "Sit down, I won't be long."

"Emily."

It was the gentleness of his voice that stopped her before she reached the bedroom door. She looked back at him. "What?"

"Are you really dreading our time together so much?"

"What do you mean?"

With two steps he was in front of her. "I'd rather not do this at all if you're going to be unhappy."

Maybe it was because she had trouble thinking clearly whenever he was close, but she couldn't imagine what he was getting at. "What has my being happy or unhappy got to do with anything?"

"Just about everything. It's going to be damned hard to spend time with you and get to know you if you're miserable."

Something like panic began to blur her vision. It was absolutely critical that she have the rest of the money. "You're thinking of backing out of our agreement?"

"That's not what I said."

"Yes, it is. More or less. I don't understand. Last night you were pushing me into the deal. You wouldn't even let me come home to pack."

"Last night I had hopes that once you made the decision, you'd relax and begin to enjoy being with me as much as I enjoy being with you."

She stiffened. "You'll have to excuse me. I've never done this sort of thing before. I don't know all the rules of conduct."

"I told you, we'll make up our own rules, and as far as I can see, the rules are changeable as we go along. But if you're so completely miserable with the setup and have such an aversion to me, then, much as I hate to admit it, there's no point in going on." He had every intention of continuing his pursuit of her, but he was probing, testing, trying to get a response from her.

She gritted her teeth together. "Take my word for it—I'm fine."

"Are you sure? Because if you're going to be unhappy the whole time—"

She gave an impatient shake of her head. "I have a lot on my mind, that's all."

"Anything I can help with?"

"No!"

He shifted his stance, his expression sharp and thoughtful. "You're not used to anyone helping you, are you?"

She gave a short, mirthless laugh. "No, I'm not."

"I didn't used to be either. No one ever offered, at least not when I really needed it. But I'm offering to help you, if you'll just let me."

She shook her head, this time more slowly and taking care to keep her gaze on him. "It's better if a person doesn't rely on someone else. That way they'll never be disappointed."

"Who's disappointed you, Emily?" he asked softly, his voice gliding along her skin like a caress.

"No one lately. I won't allow it."

He lifted his hand and lightly touched the soft curve of her cheek. His voice had prepared the way so that his touch was like a continuation of the caress. "One of these days you're going to have to let your guard down.

It's inevitable." His tone was so quiet, it was almost as if he were sharing an intimate secret with her. "And when you do, I'll be there. Until then . . ." Sliding his hand beneath her hair and around her neck, he lowered his head and lightly pressed his lips to hers.

The kiss took her by surprise. And so did the pleasure and warmth that immediately welled up inside her. The surprise was so great that at first she didn't move. She simply stood there, her head tilted back, her mind in shock, and allowed him to move his mouth over hers with a sure but gentle expertise.

Her sigh was the next surprise. It escaped from her as she parted her lips, and sounded soft and full of a wanting she didn't recognize.

She had never before wanted a man, never before felt soft. But he made her feel both emotions, emotions in their infant stages, too new to really know what they meant, too new to be frightened of.

Taking his time, he wrapped his arms around her and gathered her to him, molding her to his hard body from breast to knees. Then he delved his tongue into her mouth, scraping the velvet roughness of it against hers. The rush of feelings that filled her were staggering. Heat wound into her and coiled low in her body, making her feel strange and light-headed. But most of all she felt hot . . . and weak. If he hadn't been holding her, she might have fallen.

This wasn't what she wanted—this softness inside, as if she might actually be able to change shape and become somehow new and different. And she certainly didn't want this heat that made her forget what she was supposed to be doing and why.

She put a hand on his shoulder, intending to brace herself and prepare to push away from him, but she felt his muscles bunch beneath her palm and became fascinated with the evidence of the strength of his body. And then insidiously he deepened the kiss, opening her mouth wider with the pressure of his, delving his tongue even farther into her mouth. The heat turned to fire, and an aching started low in her body.

Desire. She had never felt desire before, and she was amazed. He was making her want him, *really* want him. She couldn't allow the kiss to continue.

Feeling foolish and clumsy, she placed her palms against his chest and tried to push, but her effort carried no strength. Then surprise came again, along with a small portion of disappointment, when he broke off the kiss and lifted his head.

Gazing down at her, he saw confusion in her eyes, and desire, and he silently cursed. The desire made him want to kiss her again, but the confusion kept him from taking what he wanted. He released his hold on her and took a step back.

Her lungs felt starved for air, but it took a great deal of concentration and effort before she finally managed to draw in a deep breath. "Sex was not part of the deal, Jay."

"That wasn't sex, Emily." He reached out and

brushed his thumb across her bottom lip, gathering up the moisture. "It was only a simple kiss." His tongue flicked over the pad of his thumb, licking at the moistness and her taste that it held.

She stared at him, aware that she was dangerously close to being spellbound.

"Do you want me to show you what sex is?" he asked, his green eyes dark as a forest at night. "Just ask, that's all you have to do."

She almost groaned aloud. She pointed an unsteady finger toward a chair. "Sit down." She moved around him to an ancient portable TV that was sitting in one corner and switched it on. "I'll try not to be long."

He watched her retreat to the next room and close the door behind her, then he turned his head to stare unseeingly at the flickering black-and-white screen.

Now he understood the innocence, he thought, and it made the sin all the more puzzling.

In the bedroom Emily sank down on her bed and dropped her head into her hands, willing the trembling in her legs to stop. Jay was right—it had only been a kiss. *Only.*

But, she assured herself, her reaction to him wasn't a disaster. Nothing had happened, not really.

He had called the kiss simple. Simple to *him* maybe. She pressed her fingers against her lips.

The kiss had involved every one of her senses and created feelings that had the power to disturb and disorder not only her priorities but her life. Simple? *No way.*

Perspective, she told herself. *Keep everything in perspective.*

The money. The money was all that was important.

And he was paying her a great deal, more than she could earn in two or even three years. Okay, then, if he wanted to kiss her occasionally, she shouldn't let it knock her off balance. His kiss hadn't hurt her, hadn't caused her pain in any way. Quite the opposite in fact.

And now that he had kissed her, she would know better how to handle herself next time. *If* there was a next time.

He had asked her if she wanted him to show her what sex was. Not a chance!

He had kissed her, and she had managed to remain whole and safe, but she could give herself no such assurances if he took her to bed. A man like Jay would leave an indelible mark on any woman he made love to, and she couldn't tolerate marks. . . .

Pulling herself together, she reached for the phone and dialed the number of the nursing home she had picked out months ago.

As soon as the administrator, Miriam Thompson, came on the line, she spoke, pitching her voice lower than the TV in the other room. "This is Emily Stanton. I was there last fall. Do you remember?"

"Yes, Miss Stanton, of course I do." The woman's voice was warm and friendly. "I remember very well. You were extremely worried and upset about your mother, but I wasn't able to help you. How are you, and how is she?"

"I'm fine, but I'm still worried about my mother. She never complains, but her situation is nearly unbearable."

"I'm sorry to hear that. I wish there was something I could do, but—"

"There is something you can do. I have some great news. I've been able to arrange my finances so that I can afford to put my mother into your home."

"That *is* great news."

"All you have to do is tell me you have a room available."

There was a pause on the other end of the line. "I'm sorry, but I'm afraid I don't. Like I told you last fall, we have a long waiting list."

Tears stung Emily's eyes. "But you *must* have something. You've *got* to have. My mother can't stay one day longer where she is. You wouldn't believe the deplorable conditions."

Miriam Thompson's sigh indicated that she could.

"I shouldn't tell you this, but most of our waiting list is for private rooms. As it happens, one of our residents who has a private room has been talking about the idea of getting a roommate. She gets lonely—"

"That would be great!" she said, her spirits soaring. Then she realized she was talking too loud and lowered her voice. "That would be perfect."

"Don't get too excited," Mrs. Thompson warned. "She's just been *talking* about it, she hasn't really made a decision. I'll tell you what, let me talk to her, and I'll get back to you."

Emily let out a pent-up breath. "Wonderful. Tell the lady that my mother may be incapacitated, but she can be good company. She just hasn't had the opportunity in the home where she is now. When can I call you back? Today?"

The older woman chuckled understandingly at Emily's urgency. "Call me back this afternoon. I'll try to have an answer for you."

"Thank you, Mrs. Thompson. You have no idea how much this means to me."

She made one more call, this one to the restaurant where she worked to tell them she wouldn't be back. Then she packed. Ten minutes later she returned to the living room holding two paper bags full of her things.

"What are these?" Jay asked, standing and taking them from her.

She shrugged. "I don't have a suitcase, so I used paper bags." A formidable frown appeared on his face. "Jay, for heaven's sake, it's no big deal. It's not so much a case of lacking the money to buy a suitcase as it is the lack of time and money for a vacation."

The frown disappeared to be replaced by an expression of curiosity. "Have you ever been on a vacation?"

"No." Not even on a family vacation when she had been a child.

He swiveled to place the paper bags on a chair, then turned back to her. "I don't take any either," he said slowly, thoughtfully. "Not really. I travel on business a great deal, and I go away for weekends quite a bit, but when I do, I always bring my work with me. Maybe you and I will have to take a vacation."

"Go on a trip together?" she asked, startled.

"Why not?"

"Well, because . . ." She groped for a reason.

He slipped one hand into his pocket, and he brushed the other over her hair. He had meant only to be reassuring, but the touch turned into a caress. "Don't worry, I'd make sure you had your own bedroom."

After experiencing his kiss, his touch barely affected her. "It's not that."

He bent his knees, bringing his eyes level with hers. "Then what is it? As long as we go and come back in the next nine days, I don't see a problem."

She did—a *huge* problem. If the lady Miriam Thompson had told her about couldn't make up her mind about whether or not she wanted a roommate, she was going to have to get out and try to find another home for her mother. And then she was going to have to oversee her transfer. "I can't go anywhere for the next couple of days. I have . . . something to take care of."

He straightened, and his expression hardened. "I thought I had bought all your time for fifty thousand dollars. Like I said, if you want more money—"

"Stop it, Jay. Try to understand."

"How can I understand something I know nothing about?"

"All you have to know is that it's something that's important to me."

"And having you all to myself is important to *me*." He caught what looked suspiciously like tears in the amber depths of her eyes. The sight seemed somehow obscene, like a splash of paint defacing an exquisite work of art. With a silent curse he gave in. "Okay, Emily, how long are we talking?"

"I really can't say." She held up her hand as she saw his expression darken again. "I know that my time is supposed to be yours, but I'll make it up to you somehow."

"Really?" His eyes narrowed with interest. "And how do you propose to do that?"

Her composure suffered beneath his scrutiny. "I don't know right now. Maybe I'll tack some time on at the end of the nine days. Would you like that? Another full day and night? Two?"

In a movement so quick she didn't see it coming, he reached for her and pulled her against him. "Maybe," he said with a rough growl. "But for now I have a better idea. Give me something on account."

The fire burning in his eyes warned her, but she had only a split second to catch her breath before he brought his mouth down on hers in a crushing kiss.

Instantaneous pleasure, instantaneous heat, instantaneous want. All the feelings she had felt in their first kiss came rushing back, but this time a hundred times more intense, a hundred times more powerful. Naturally, easily, she sank against him and gave herself up to the vivid sensations of warmth and desire.

Every day at the florist shop she was surrounded by the heavenly fragrances of the flowers, but she didn't think she had ever smelled anything as wonderful as Jay. His scent was clean, exotically sexual, and erotically tantalizing, and it made her knees weak and her heart hammer like a wild thing.

His body, too, was a wondrous thing made up of steellike strength and a hard ridge of desire that pressed against her middle. She might be an innocent when it came to sex, but she knew what that pressure against her meant. He had told her that he wanted her, but being told and being shown were two very different things. The physical evidence of his desire shook the foundation of her resistance to him. A fever invaded her body, gripping every vital part, and she pressed closer to him.

His tongue had been in her mouth before, but this time the act seemed shatteringly intimate, like something private and secret shared by only the two of them. And worse, she loved everything about the invasion. Part of him was deep inside her, and she opened her mouth wider to take more of him in, arching against him, imitating the act of sex with her own tongue.

It was a safe way to experience him, she told herself, but then she heard the strange sounds of wanting that seemed to be escaping from *her*. Safe? She was kidding herself. A mighty need was tingling and growing throughout her, and her breasts were swelling and aching. Used to his kisses now, her body wanted more.

But once again he was the one who ended the kiss.

For a moment she could only stand there and stare at him. Then her mind started to work again.

Perspective.

This time it was harder to find. But she tried, oh, how she tried.

So she had come undone in his arms. So he could make her want more than just his kisses and his touches. So what?

He was a sophisticated man, experienced at making love to women. It was obvious he viewed a kiss as a harmless diversion, and she should too. She *would not* humiliate herself by acting like an outraged virgin.

She swayed. His hand snaked out to grasp her upper arm and steady her.

"Let's wait and see how long it takes you to handle the matter," he muttered, his eyes glittering darkly. "Then I'll decide how much you owe me."

THREE

If she had ever had an idea of what a butler should be—and Emily couldn't remember that she had—John would be it, she decided, watching him preside over their lunch. He was unobtrusive, discreet, and exceedingly polite, but his presence made her feel as if she were using the wrong fork, even though she knew she wasn't.

With her mind on her mother and her body still recovering from Jay's kisses, John was almost more than she could deal with. The small amount of food she had managed to get down lay like a concrete lump in her stomach. She was ready to say she didn't want any more, when she happened to catch the glint of reassurance and humor in Jay's eyes.

"John," he said casually, "we'll serve ourselves the rest of the meal."

Disapproval was etched in every trim line of John's

body, but he merely said, "Very well, sir."

"You shouldn't let him get to you," Jay said after they were alone. "The trick is to treat him like he's a panel of wallpaper."

She looked at him with disbelief. "You're kidding."

He shook his head. "I know it sounds rude and maybe even cruel, but believe me it's his heart's desire to be regarded as such."

"Why on earth would he want to be regarded as a panel of wallpaper?"

"Because he believes a truly good butler should expedite his employer's every wish in a way that is as inconspicuous as possible. If he is noticed too much, he feels he has failed."

"Doesn't that strike you as a trifle weird?"

He shrugged. "It did at first, but I work very hard, and appreciate the way he and his wife take care of my home. They make things infinitely easy for me."

She tried to imagine herself in the same situation, where one or more persons devoted themselves to smoothing out the bumps in her life so that she didn't have to worry about ordinary things such as taking out the trash on the proper day and washing clothes at ten o'clock at night so that she'd have something clean to wear the next morning. She tried to imagine it, but she couldn't.

"John's wife is a different personality type. You haven't met her yet. Cooking is an obsession with her. She sometimes stays in her kitchen for days at time, and when she does, she usually ends up with enough food to feed a small country."

"What does she do with it all?"

"She puts some of it in the freezer, and the rest she gives to neighbors and homeless shelters."

"And you don't mind that she's giving away your food?"

"Not as long as it's not wasted and I get fed. What would you like to do this afternoon?"

She blinked at the abrupt change of subject. "I'm not sure I *can* do anything. There's something I may have to take care of."

A muscle moved in his jaw, but his tone remained even. "Does this something entail your leaving the house?"

"I don't know yet."

"Well, Emily, then who does? I certainly don't."

Anger flashed in her eyes at his barely veiled sarcasm. "I'll let you know," she snapped, then instantly regretted it. She couldn't afford to antagonize him to the point that he would back out of their deal. On the other hand, she instinctively chafed at dominance of any kind. Unfortunately their agreement lent itself to the very control she found so hard to tolerate. The saving grace was that their deal had an end date to it. At least she wouldn't be stuck with Jay for the rest of her life.

Stuck.

She glanced down the table at him. His face was all

angles and planes, his body a study in relaxed power, his green-eyed gaze full of intensity. He fascinated her. He was doing nothing more than eating lunch, yet he gave off waves of sexuality that seemed to her just this side of being untamed.

"Are you all right?" Jay asked. "You're staring at me as if you're waiting for me to sprout horns."

Actually, she realized with a jolt, she was staring at him as if he were a piece of dark, rich chocolate, just as the woman with the ivory-tinted bosom had last night. And like the woman, she recognized inherent danger when she saw it. "I'm fine." Unable to eat another bite, she lifted the linen napkin from her lap and placed it by the side of her plate.

Stuck with him for the rest of her life. There would be any number of women ready to call her crazy for her attitude, but there was nothing she could do about her feelings. Her instinct to rebel against control went bone deep and was unalterable. That instinct accounted for her hesitation to accept his deal in the first place, despite her great need for the money.

But in the next week and a half she had to make a conscious effort to comply. It was her job to do what he said. "I'm sorry."

"For what?"

"For snapping at you."

He sighed. "Don't censor yourself, Emily. Don't watch every word you speak."

She shrugged. "The very least I can do for five

thousand a day is to be pleasant. You said it yourself—you don't want me to be unhappy, and I can understand that. It would be no fun to have a morose companion."

He dropped his head to the side and rubbed his temple. "Boy, am I ever going to have a hard time winning with you."

"Winning? It's your deal, your money—you hold all the cards. What's the problem?"

"I'm not sure." He sighed again, this time more heavily. "Look, I know you're finding this awkward, Emily. It *is* awkward. But it only has to be as awkward as you and I make it. You want to do this in the right way? Throw out your mental list of dos and don'ts. Be yourself with me. And most of all be honest."

"I haven't lied to you."

He smiled wryly. "Maybe not, but you haven't told me the whole truth on anything either."

He was right. She had known from the beginning that he could see through lies, so she had compromised and told him half-truths. He had seen those for what they were too. "Your money doesn't give you the right to probe into every corner of my life."

"No, you're right, it doesn't. Which I guess means I'll have to be satisfied with whatever crumbs you give me."

His phrasing struck her as odd. "You'll *have* to be?"

He nodded. "If I want you. And it seems that I still do."

It was a very low-key statement. His voice held little intensity. But heat crawled through her veins, firing nerve endings as it went.

To be wanted by Jay Barrett was a powerful stimulant.

Unbidden, an image came into her mind of a woman in bed with Jay. They were both naked. He was on top of her, her legs were wrapped around his back, and he was driving deeply into her.

She lifted a glass of ice water to her lips and drank, but it didn't cool her inflamed senses. The woman's moans of ecstasy sounded in her ears. And then suddenly she felt a heated pressure low in her womb, almost as if she were the woman in her mind and Jay was actually buried deep inside her.

She sat the glass of water down and put a hand to her mouth, pressing her fingers hard against her lips until the image vanished from her mind and the impulse to moan in ecstasy went away.

She cast a surreptitious glance at her watch and noted she had to wait at least a couple of more hours before she could call Mrs. Thompson. "I should see to the flower arrangements. They'll be needing fresh water."

He leaned back in his chair. "You will let me know, won't you, when you think you'll have time for me?"

"I'll be sure and do that," she said pleasantly, determinedly ignoring his sarcasm.

"Good, because I'd like to take you for a drive in the

country. I'd like to sit in a darkened movie theater with you and hold your hand. I'd like to slide inside you and never, ever leave."

Her hand jerked, and the water goblet went flying.

He smiled slowly. "The latter of course," he said, his voice deep and thick, "is subject to your approval."

She barely heard him. Horrified at what she'd done, she snatched up her napkin and frantically dabbed at the water-soaked tablecloth.

In a leisurely manner he rose, strolled the length of the table, lifted the tablecloth, and slid his napkin between the wet linen and the table. "There," he said, kneeling beside her. "That should help things until John comes to clear away the dishes."

Her eyes showed apprehension. "But shouldn't you call him in now? The water will mark the wood."

"If it does, John will have the piece refinished. In any case it's nothing for you to worry about."

"I'm so sorry."

"For what?" He reached out and smoothed his fingers over the furrows in her brow. "It was an accident. You didn't do it on purpose. And even if you did, it's not a big thing."

"I didn't do it on purpose, but—"

"But what?"

"Nothing." She couldn't tell him about the time she had knocked over a glass at the dinner table and her stepfather had flown into a rage that had ended with him beating her mother. Her mother had instilled in

her the need to be quiet and still so as not to antagonize her stepfather, and so she had sat on her bed and
listened to her mother's cries and wanted to die.

"Emily?"

The gentleness in his voice drew her back to the
present. She liked his gentleness, she realized. And
she was thrilled by his desire for her, deep down in
some very basic female part of her that had never been
touched before. And she was afraid, not of his gentleness or his desire but of something she couldn't quite
put her finger on. "I wish you wouldn't say things like
you did." Damn, she hated to sound prudish, but she
had done it again.

"You mean about slipping inside you?"

"Exactly." Agitated, she combed her fingers through
her hair, disrupting its style. "You know it's not going
to happen. I told you it wasn't."

He lightly stroked the shining strands of her hair
back into place. "I have a tendency to say what's on
my mind, Emily. Besides, I like to see your reaction.
It's one of the rare times I can actually tell what you're
thinking. Then, and when I kiss you."

He stood, and clasping her hand, he drew her from
the chair to her feet. "I'll go do a little work while you
tend to the flowers."

"Really?"

"You look so surprised."

"I am. I expected more of an argument to try to
stop me from going anywhere this afternoon."

His eyes glinted with a light she was instantly wary of.

"I figure the more you owe me, the better off I'll be."

Working with flowers soothed her. It always did. She loved nothing more than to wade into a sea of branches, leaves, and scented blossoms and arrange them so that the whole was even more beautiful than the part. She never forced her arrangements into uniform configurations. Rather she loved to be spontaneous, adding volume, texture, and color until some inner instinct told her the arrangement was complete.

As she moved around the house, refreshing each bouquet with clean water and pulling out any wilting blossoms, she studied Jay's house.

Jay was a detail man. She had known that when he had come in to order the flowers for his party. Normally a man with Jay's money and position would use a secretary or a party planner for such a chore, even if the florist was one he had never used before, as Harriet had been. But Jay had come himself.

Now she saw the same attention invested in his home. As she wandered from room to room, she realized that though the wing of the house where last night's party had been held was formal, the rest was more relaxed. These were the rooms where Jay actually lived, where he retreated from the world.

Retreat. What a funny word for her to think of. To her mind Jay was the kind of man who would never retreat from anything.

Still, Jay himself had chosen and placed each piece, though she wasn't sure how she knew that. *Comfortable*, *gentle*, and *sensual* were the words she would use to describe his home. Color was used subtly with the occasional, but completely appropriate dramatic touch.

He had taken diverse pieces of furniture and objects of art—an eclectic mix of Oriental, French, English, and American styles—and created a cocoon of serenity.

Even more amazing was the fact that it looked as if the same family had lived there for a very long time, collecting well-loved items along the way. The art compelled you to enjoy. The sofas and chairs invited you to sink into them, the tables lured you to put your feet up. Not that *she* would dare.

Eventually she found herself at the back of the house in a cozy room whose wide windows overlooked a sweeping lawn and a multihued garden that featured a living bouquet of everything from hollyhocks and delphiniums to roses and tulips. A fire burned in the fireplace, and Jay was sitting on the couch, reading a newspaper.

"I thought you were in your study."

He put down the paper and gave her a lazy smile. "I was for a while, but I decided to come in here and wait for you to find me."

"I wasn't looking for you, I—"

"Never mind. Come sit down and talk to me."

She gestured toward the door, indicating other rooms. "I haven't finished with the flowers yet."

"You've done enough for today. The rest can wait until tomorrow, or the day after."

The room was inviting with its cushy, plump furniture and the spill of sunlight through the wide windows. And then there was Jay, sitting on an apricot-silk couch that was lined with pillows. An instantaneous impression flashed in her mind: He was the only hard thing in the room.

She glanced at her watch. "I can sit down for a few minutes."

His expression turned wry. "I'm grateful for whatever time you can give me, Emily."

Her eyes narrowed. "Let's don't start that again."

"Whatever you say."

She dropped into the chair across from him and was immediately enveloped by comfort. "What is it about you and flowers? I found arrangements of mine that I didn't realize you had bought."

"I think flowers are one of the things that make a house a home."

"One of the things?"

"A fire is another. I usually have fires even in the summer."

Her lips curved into what was almost a smile. "I bet your air-conditioning bill is spectacular."

His eyes went to her lips, and he wondered if she

would ever smile for him. And he wondered what a real smile from her would do to him, considering the fact that even the merest hint of one made him want to pull her to him and kiss her until she promised never to stop smiling at him.

She could feel his gaze on her skin, burning her everywhere it touched. What did one do for first-degree burns? she wondered. Ice? Salve?

She glanced away toward the garden beyond the window. Ten acres in the middle of North Dallas—a rarity that came with a high price. "I was told this is the old Rustin estate."

"It's mine now."

"I realize that, but you probably know even better than I do that this is an old-money section of Dallas, and people who have grown up in the area label the houses here according to who owned it in the past."

"Then you're from around here?"

"No, but people talk and I listen."

He waited, and when she didn't elaborate, he said, "There's not a twig or a stone that I haven't changed in the seven years that I've lived here. As far as I'm concerned, that makes it mine."

Her lips curved again, the merest hint of amusement. "You sound very possessive."

His gaze went to her lips. "I am—about some things."

"Well, you have every right to be proud. Your house is beautiful. It's very . . . I don't know . . . *soft*."

"That's exactly the effect I wanted. I do battle daily outside these walls. When I come home, I want to be surrounded by softness."

"That's interesting."

"Why? Don't I seem like the kind of man who would crave softness?"

She absently combed her fingers through her hair. "No. You seem like a consummate businessman who won't let anyone or anything stand in the way of getting what he wants."

"You've just defined a ruthless man. Is that the way you see me?"

"You have to admit you wouldn't take no for an answer when it came to getting me to spend time with you."

"I admit it. But you haven't been hurt in the process, have you? In fact you're going to come out way ahead."

The idea of taking the money from him still made her want to cringe, but, she thought, she didn't owe anyone an apology, least of all herself.

Her silence drew further probing. "Do you still think of me as ruthless, Emily? I mean, since you've been with me, is ruthlessness the sum total of what you expect of me?"

No. There were his touches that were disarmingly gentle, and his kisses of fire that made her go soft and hot. Just this once, she wondered, could she lie to him? "Yes."

"I'm sorry to hear that," he said, his tone flat. "Your opinion of me must be extremely low."

"Does it matter what I think?"

"A great deal."

No. She couldn't lie to him. "You're very gentle with me."

"Pardon me?"

Restless, she stood up and moved around the room. "You've always been gentle with me, even during the time when you weren't sure I'd agree to stay with you."

"Why wouldn't I be gentle with you, Emily?" he asked with honest curiosity. "I can't imagine being any other way with you."

She shrugged. "It's not really important."

"Meaning you wouldn't care if I was rough with you?"

"No, I don't mean that at all. But you certainly don't have to be as careful with me as you are. It's almost as if you think I were a piece of glass that might break. I won't, you know. I can take a level above gentleness."

"Maybe so, but I don't think I could."

A heated shiver of indeterminable origin raced through her, and she wrapped her arms around herself. "You're a strange man."

He smiled. "Yes, I know."

She stopped in front of a sculpture, an exquisitely detailed head of a little boy. She was captivated by his expression of complete and utter happiness. Almost expecting to feel the softness of his hair, she laid a hand on the child's curly head. "This is the way all children should look," she murmured.

"I agree. In fact it was his expression that attracted me to him." He rose and went to the fireplace, where he pulled a log from a wicker basket and tossed it onto the fire.

She kept her hand on the child's head, deriving a sense of peace from it. But then she drew away. Jay's presence was too electric for her ever to be able to relax with him. "This piece of sculpture aside, do you buy art for its intrinsic value or because of how it makes you feel?"

He straightened, slipped his hands into his pockets, and gazed thoughtfully at her. "What do you think?"

She said what she wanted to hear. "For its value."

He grinned. "If I want to keep my ego intact, I'm really going to have to stop asking you for your opinion of me."

"Well?"

"For how it makes me feel."

Deep down inside, she realized, she had known what his answer would be. Without really thinking about it, she returned her hand to the child's sculpted hair. "Then tell me about the painting of the longhorns in your study."

"I admire their breed. They're able to endure despite great odds."

"But you have it hanging opposite a real Monet. I

mean, I *assume* it's real. I know some people buy copies, but—"

"It's real. And the reason I have it opposite the longhorns is that it balances the rugged starkness of the other painting."

After a moment's consideration she said, "You have the eye of an artist."

His mouth twisted ruefully. "I don't suppose that's a compliment."

"A fact."

He moved to her and took her free hand in his. "Then let me tell you another fact. You also have the eye of an artist. It's in every flower arrangement you make."

"No," she said, shaking her head, rejecting what he had said. "I simply stick flowers in a vase."

"It's more than that, and you know it."

He had a way of looking at her that made her feel as if he were absorbing her. Like now. Even though she had been keeping track of the time, almost counting the minutes until she could call Miriam Thompson again, she extracted her hand from his and pointedly glanced at her watch. "I have to make a phone call."

"Use my study. You'll have privacy there."

"Thank you."

"Don't thank me. While you're staying here, I want you to consider the house yours."

"Be serious, Jay. You've seen where I live. This

house is as alien an environment to me as the moon would be."

"You can get used to it. I did, and I've lived in places that would make your apartment look like a palace."

"You're making that up."

"Not even a little bit."

As she made her way to his study, she tried to picture Jay living in something smaller than her apartment, but she couldn't. This house suited him perfectly.

At the study door she stopped and looked across the room at the telephone sitting on the desk. Thoughts of Jay left her as dread leeched the warmth from her body.

Everything depended on the lady with the private room. What if she didn't want her mother as a roommate? Even though she had the money, she'd have to start her search for another place immediately. And how long could she reasonably expect Jay to wait for her? She was already pressing her luck as it was.

And if he called off the deal . . .

The dread grew worse, and her heart pounded.

She started across the room.

When Emily walked back into the room, Jay's breath caught in his throat. Her amber eyes were glittering like stars, and her skin glowed with an inner luminosity.

She was smiling.

And not because of him, he realized.

"I have to go out," Emily said, barely able to keep still. She was so elated, she felt like dancing, like shouting, "Hooray." She could still hear Miriam Thompson's voice.

The name of the lady I spoke to you about is Elizabeth Horton, and she is delighted with the idea of a roommate. We'll be ready for your mother as soon as you can make arrangements for her transfer.

She was already busy compiling a mental list of all the things she needed to do.

"Is it a man?"

She looked up at Jay blankly. "What?"

He reached out to trace the outline of her lips. "You were smiling when you came in. Was it because of a man?"

She gave a short laugh of disbelief. "A *man*? Right, and pigs fly."

He felt the tension ease from his muscles. "Is the idea of a man in your life so foreign to you?"

She shook her head impatiently. "Look, I need to go. We can talk this evening."

"Wait." He caught her arm. "Something has changed with you. You're happier. Tell me why."

"I received some good news, some *really* good news." Once again it was the truth, but not the complete truth, and she had a feeling he knew it. Impulsively she reached out and touched his arm, but then, shocked at herself, she immediately jerked away. "I'm not sure how long this will take, but I should be back by dinnertime." Before he could question her further, she started to back out of the door. "I'll see you—"

"Emily?"

"What?"

"Drive carefully."

She stopped and looked back at him, an odd expression on her face. "Why would you say a thing like that?"

"You're obviously excited about something, and I just wanted to remind you to pay attention to your driving. I wouldn't want you to get into a wreck."

She nodded, understanding now. "Don't worry. Once I get this settled, I promise nothing else will interfere with our time together. See you in a little bit."

Jay stared after her, more frustrated than he had ever been in his life. She didn't understand. His reason for worrying about her had been completely unselfish and had nothing to do with their time together. Hell, *he* didn't even understand it. Why had he ever settled for ten days? It wouldn't begin to be enough time to break through to her, nor would it be enough time to figure out why she affected him so.

Just where in the sweet hell had she gone, anyway? He was both wild with curiosity and eaten up with jealousy. The question was, At whom or what should he aim the jealousy? He had no idea whether it was a person or a situation that had pulled her away from him, and at this moment he wondered if it even mattered. The point was she had left, and he quite frankly didn't like it.

Unfortunately he had no choice but to bide his time. Something or someone had compelled her to leave him, and she didn't trust him enough to tell him why. As much as he wanted to do otherwise, he wasn't about to compound the problem by following her.

FOUR

"You're going to love the place, Mom," Emily said, keeping her voice low so that she wouldn't disturb the other women who shared the ward. She was sitting beside her mother's bed, holding to her mother's lips the straw she had placed in a protein-and-vitamin drink. She waited until she had taken a small sip. She worried about her mother's poor appetite. On her way to the nursing home she had stopped at a health-food store and splurged on the expensive drink, along with a piece of fresh fruit.

"Are you sure you can afford this, Emily?"

"Yes, I told you. The florist shop where I work is doing really well, and I got a raise. Besides, the new place doesn't cost that much more than this one." Her conscience was completely clear as she told the lie. Her mother had had to face enough reality and truth in her life. If the lie gave her peace of mind, so be it.

With a loving hand Emily reached up and smoothed the older woman's snow-white hair back from her face. Even though her mother was only in her early fifties, she had prematurely aged.

She heard the fingers of her mother's right hand rubbing against the coarse sheet. She put the glass on the floor, then covered her mother's hand with hers. "There's nothing to worry about. In fact I want you to be excited. You'll be getting better care and the opportunity to work with a physical therapist. You should be able to regain your strength in no time at all."

"It's not fair to you, Emily." Her gaze rested on her daughter. "You're so young. You've got your whole life in front of you. I'm such a burden, and you shouldn't have to—"

"Hush," Emily said gently. "I don't want to hear it. You're not a burden. I love you. Besides, you'd do the same for me, wouldn't you?"

"You know I would."

"Then let me take care of you." Emily tore off a piece of banana and offered it to her. "Just think," she said lightly. "They're going to have food that tastes like *real* food at the new place, and their personnel will have the time to help you eat."

"That's good. Then you won't have to come every day like you've been doing."

"I've *wanted* to visit you." It was true, but it was also true her visits had been the only way she could be certain that her mother was getting at least one full meal a day. The staff simply had too many people to take care of to spend the proper amount of time needed to ensure that each patient ate enough. She offered the drink again. "Speaking of visiting—after I get you settled tomorrow, I may not be able to come and see you as often as I usually do this next week." Continuing to sip, her mother looked at her expectantly. "I thought I'd take a few days off from work and go on a little vacation with a girlfriend." When she saw her mother's face light up, she knew she had made up the right excuse.

"Oh, Emily, that's wonderful. You'll be able to rest. Sometimes you come in here looking so tired. I worry. . . ."

"But you're going to stop that now, aren't you? Things are looking up for us, Mom, and you're going to get better, I just know it."

"I hope so," she said. "For both our sakes. Emily?"

"What?"

"Am I going to be using the false last name in the new place?"

"Yes, Mom. It's safer that way."

She nodded, and when Emily held out the drink to her again, she finished it without another word.

Jay opened the front door a few seconds after Emily rang the doorbell.

"Is it John's night off?" she asked, entering.

"It's my door, Emily," he said, slamming it behind her. "I can damn well open it if I want to."

The slicing edge of his voice told her what she had already anticipated. He was unhappy that she had been gone so long.

"Are you done?" he asked. "Is it over?"

She clenched her hands in front of her and braced for the full onslaught of his anger. "No."

He stared at her.

"Tomorrow, Jay. Tomorrow I'll be done." Resigned, she waited for the inevitable explosion.

"All right." He looked down at his feet, seeming to study his black-leather loafers with great interest. Finally he returned his gaze to her. "Would you like to go out tonight?"

It was several moments before she fully absorbed his question. *And* his calm mood. "Jay, I don't have any clothes that would be appropriate for a place you would frequent."

"How do you know? How do you know where I go and what I do?"

"Well, it's fairly easy for me to see—"

"No, Emily, you only *think* it's easy, because in your mind you've already neatly categorized me."

He was both right and wrong. She had mentally classified him as a stereotypical rich man because it was what she very much wanted to believe.

But the *scars*. She had seen them in him from the beginning, and they wouldn't let her easily dismiss him.

Traumas layered scar upon scar deep in a person's soul, and she had great respect for anyone who bore such scars. But to examine his too closely would indicate real interest on her part, and interest was something she was trying hard to avoid.

"Have you looked in the closet in your bedroom?" he asked, his quiet voice breaking into the silence.

"Yes." The closet held about half a dozen new outfits. "They're very nice, but I don't feel comfortable wearing clothes you bought for me."

"Why not? I picked them out for you. I'd like to see you in them."

She sighed. She was so happy about the new nursing home for her mother, she should probably give in to him on this one. After all, when it was all said and done, what difference would it really make? When she left here, she would leave the clothes behind as easily as she would Jay.

"Now that I think about it, it's understandable that you'd like me to dress appropriately. I'll be going places as your date, and you'll want me to look nice. So, okay. What would you like me to wear tonight?"

He muttered a harsh curse beneath his breath. "You know, Emily, I feel like I'm beating my head against a wall with you."

She had no idea what he meant. What's more, she didn't want to know. "I'm sorry. That must hurt."

"Like hell."

She considered his anything-but-light retort and

the hard, dark glint in his eyes. He was a complicated man, too complex to understand easily. Prudently she decided to return the conversation to its original track. "Getting back to the clothes . . ."

"Those clothes haven't got a thing to do with any so-called desire on my part for you to be dressed appropriately, whatever the hell that means. I simply wanted to buy you something nice, and I thought you would enjoy them."

"You're paying me enough money, Jay. You don't have to buy me presents too."

A muscle flexed in his jaw. "*Fine. Great.* Then that's settled. Did you bring any jeans?"

"Jeans? Yes—"

He grasped her upper arms and turned her toward the staircase. "Go change into your jeans and a T-shirt, and I'll see you back down here in about ten minutes."

"Are you comfortable?" Jay asked, handing her a small bottle of sparkling water and settling back against one of the two canvas ground chairs he had set up on top of a large quilt.

"Very." In a chair identical to his she leaned back, stretched her legs out in front of her, and took a swallow of water. He had offered her wine, but she had refused.

About fifty yards away from them, a jazz ensemble played on a temporary stage set up in the middle of a park. Beyond the stage the lights of the Dallas skyline stabbed upward through the darkness of the sky. A cool, refreshing breeze filtered through the tall oak trees that lined the park's edge. Emily couldn't remember a more pleasant night. But then she also couldn't remember the last time she'd taken the time to even notice a night, *any* night, no matter what it looked like.

"Do you do this often?" she asked curiously, screwing the top back onto the bottle of water and setting it beside her. "Come to the park to hear concerts, I mean." They were at the back of the crowd, far enough away from the stage so that they could enjoy the music and also talk quietly. Between them and the stage, people of all ages reclined on the grass or blankets, chatting, drinking, and eating from picnic baskets they had brought with them.

"I try to make as many performances as I can. I have season tickets to the symphony, but I find more often than not I end up giving away the tickets. Coming to the park is easier. I can get here in five minutes, and anything I happen to have on is fine. It's an enjoyable way for me to relax."

"It is nice," she admitted, realizing that her own tension seemed to be gradually lessening. Tomorrow her mother would be in the new place, tomorrow she would start getting the help she had badly needed for so long. It was an answer to a prayer.

Still, she couldn't allow herself to relax completely. If she had learned nothing else in life, it was that catastrophe could strike when you least expected it.

"Unfortunately this particular concert series happens only in late spring, and then for only a few weeks. But I try to make as many performances as I can. There's something liberating about sitting out under the stars."

She tilted her head back so that she could gaze up at the sky, sending her hair cascading over the chair almost to the ground. "I don't see any stars."

With an almost compulsive need he reached for a handful of her hair and let it sift through his fingers. "It was only a figure of speech, but the stars are up there. It's just that the lights of the city are too bright for us to see them."

"But if we can't see them, are they really up there?"

He chuckled. "Is this a question like, If a tree falls in a forest, does it make a sound?"

She nodded. "I guess it is."

"So, what do you think?"

"I'd like to think a tree falling would make a sound. It would be a shame if it didn't. Otherwise nothing would be accomplished by the tree falling. It would be like denying that it ever existed. I'd also like to think the stars are really up there. . . ."

He took her hand in his. "I tell you what we'll do. We'll drive out to the country one evening. Unless it's a cloudy night, you'll see lots of stars."

"I've never seen more than a few stars at a time," she said, her tone unconsciously wistful, "and then they're never very bright."

"That must mean you've always lived in or near a city. Either that or somewhere where the weather is often bad."

"Yes." The saxophonist had taken off on a solo, blowing notes hot enough to put smoke in the air. Near them she saw a middle-aged man take the hand of a woman Emily assumed was his wife. The two of them had the look of a couple who had been together many years. They appeared comfortable and blissfully happy with each other.

Across the way she saw a good-looking man in his early twenties put his arm around the girl Emily guessed was his girlfriend and pull her against him.

From Emily's viewpoint everyone appeared so normal, as if their lives were uncomplicated and being happy and relaxed was an everyday occurrence to them. Suddenly she felt overwhelmingly sad. Did normality really exist? And if it did, why had it never touched her life?

But then again, she reflected wearily, now wasn't the time to feel sorry for herself. For the first time in a long time, things were looking up. She might have resisted Jay from the beginning. To a point she might still be resisting him. But she had a great deal to thank him for.

She forced her mind to another, more impersonal subject. "Look at that skyline," she said, pointing. "Each new building is taller than the last, and this area is so flat, you can see them for miles."

"Are you used to flat terrain?"

"Sure. Most of Texas is flat."

"Then you were raised in Texas?"

It was a casual question, but it was also a blatant attempt at probing. She glanced over at him, but said nothing.

He smiled. "That's very good, Emily, the way you have of not giving away anything about yourself."

The breeze ruffled the ends of his hair. The lights that ringed the park, along with the distant lights from the stage and the city, were dim by the time they reached them, but they cast shadows onto his face, inexplicably making it more compelling. Sometimes she actually found it difficult to stop looking at him. "What difference does it make?"

"It doesn't make a bit of difference. So tell me."

"Yes, I was raised in Texas. Yes, it was flat."

He drew her hand to his body, holding it against his chest. The gesture warmed her, and she hadn't even realized she was cold.

"There now," he said, "telling me that didn't hurt so much, did it?"

"No." Because she hadn't told him anything important about herself. "I wouldn't let you hurt me, Jay."

Her tone was so solemn, he had to fight the urge to gather her into his arms and ask her what it was she was so afraid of. "Good for you. Not that I would hurt you."

"Maybe you wouldn't mean to, but the thing is, I don't think you know your own strength."

He shifted closer to her. "Are you talking about physical strength? Emily, I would never—"

"No," she said quickly, surprising herself. "No, I wasn't talking about physical strength. We talked about this earlier, and I told you—you treat me as if I'm made of glass."

"Then what *are* you talking about?"

She glanced away and found herself gazing at the young man, who still had his arm around his girlfriend. "Do you see that young couple over there?"

"Yes."

"I wonder if they'll still be together in twenty-five years, or if in a few years he'll break her heart?"

"*He?* Why did you automatically pick him out to be the one to do the hurting? What about her? She might be the one to break his heart."

"I guess."

With his free hand he cupped her chin and turned her face toward him. "Who's broken your heart?" he asked softly. "What man has hurt you so much, you automatically think that every man will?"

He was so close, she thought she could feel his breath on her face. She could certainly smell him. Tantalizingly male and earthily sensual, his was the kind of scent that could make a woman think longingly of endless nights and tangled sheets. She shook her head to rid it of the image. "There's been no one."

He remembered their first kiss and her innocence. "No one? You're a beautiful woman, Emily. I can't be the first man to want you."

No, but he was the first man tenacious enough to make her notice him, the first who wouldn't go away when she told him to. And he was the first man who'd gotten this far, this close. Once again she told him part of a truth. "You're the first man ever to offer me money for my companionship."

"It was creative thinking at its best," he said without even a hint of humor. "I should get an A for originality."

"Don't forget audacity. Or even lack of principle."

Hell, yes, he thought. He possessed all those things and more. He wouldn't have survived otherwise. And he wouldn't be beside her now. "Then I suppose I'm lucky, because despite the fact that I'm such an unprincipled bastard, you saw fit to grace me with your company."

"It was for your money, Jay. Nothing else."

His eyes narrowed at her flat statement. He was beginning to hate the whole idea of the money. The first time she'd refused to go out with him, he should have walked away. True, he hadn't been used to a woman telling him no. But an even stronger truth was that she had immediately captivated him to the point that he had been willing to do anything, promise anything. . . .

"Is the money really all you want?"

"Yes, it's all I want."

"You sound so hard."

"I am."

"Maybe to some extent, but there's also a softness about you too. You're just very good at hiding it." He held her gaze with his until finally she looked away. "Aren't you going to argue with me?"

"It wouldn't do any good. You've made up your mind."

"And you're not going to try to change it?" he asked with a touch against her chin that had her looking at him again.

He was too close, his lips too near hers. And she remembered more than she should of their kisses. In fact her lips were *tingling* with the memory. "Why should I bother changing your mind? We aren't going to be together that long."

"You know, Emily, I don't think I've been terribly unreasonable in this deal of ours, do you?"

There was something new in his voice that made her eye him warily. "No."

"In fact it's my opinion that I've been pretty under-standing."

He was angry, she realized. Quietly, fiercely angry. "You have."

"Then do something for me."

She tensed, unsure of what to expect, but knowing that whatever it was wouldn't be good. "What?"

"When you're with me, put the damn money out of your mind. Make me think you like me, even if it's only a little."

He leaned forward and pressed his lips to hers. There was nothing overly sexual about the kiss, just a simple touch of his lips, a light pressure. But his lips were warm and firm, and her heart thudded against her chest wall as pleasure seared through her veins. Several long, burning seconds later, he lifted his head, and his eyes were glittering darkly.

"When I kiss you, I'd like to think you're enjoying it as much as I am. Even if you're not, make me believe it."

That would be no problem, she thought, her breath catching in her throat. Her response to him was genuine. There was no question of make-believe on her part.

He swept fingers through her hair to cup the back of her head. "Every time I kiss you, I have this feeling that I'm drowning in a pool of hot honey." His fingers tightened on the back of her head. "And that's probably one of the stupidest, most nonsensical things I've ever said. But it's also the absolute truth, and because it is, I would really like to know if you feel anywhere near the same way."

With the sensation of his lips still on hers, there was no question of a half-truth. "Yes," she breathed.

"Sweet heaven, you make me want to wrap your scent around me and gorge myself on your taste until

I can't take in anymore. Another nonsensical statement that's also true. And you know what—I don't think I'd ever get to the point where I couldn't take in any more of you. I don't think I could ever have enough of you." He bent toward her and touched the tip of his tongue to one side of her mouth, then, leaving moisture and fire, swept his tongue across her lips as if she were an ice-cream cone.

The music had receded until all she could hear was Jay's voice and her pounding heart. Disoriented, weak, she forgot about the night sky, the people, the world.

"What do you think?" he asked huskily, his mouth now at the base of her ear, nibbling. "How do you like the way I taste?"

Desperate to regain her equilibrium, she attempted to rid herself of all trace of him. Her tongue darted out to lick her lips, but all she succeeded in doing was picking up his taste.

"Well?" he asked, his voice low and harsh. "Do you need more to decide?"

His lips came back to hers, touching lightly, just enough to awaken nerve endings and send them pulsing. Her mouth opened. He took the invitation and delved his tongue deep inside, boldly seeking out hidden places he had never been before. Whatever small resistance might have lingered in her shattered as if it had never been, and she gave herself up totally to the experience.

It didn't matter that somehow she was now lying

on the quilt, facing him, and that the weight of one of his legs was over hers. It didn't matter that he was cupping her breast or that her fingers, seemingly with a mind of their own, were awkwardly unbuttoning his shirt. All that mattered was deepening the kiss until she couldn't open her mouth any wider or thrust her tongue any deeper. All that mattered was pressing against him, letting her hands splay across his chest, thrusting her pelvis against the hard ridge of his lower body.

She had a need inside her that before now had been unknown to her. It was like a hunger that had to be fed, an emptiness that had to be filled, an ache that had to be assuaged.

She heard Jay whisper something, but didn't understand what he was saying. She felt his hands on her arms lightly pushing, but couldn't comprehend what he was doing. She was mindless. She was on fire. She was in great need.

"We've got to stop."

This time she heard his roughly spoken words, but her fevered mind blocked their meaning. She threaded her fingers up into his hair, relishing the silky texture.

In a quick, abrupt move Jay rolled away from her, and she was left bathed in cool air and even colder rejection.

A cry of protest rose to her lips. His eyes were closed, and his chest was rising and falling with deep breaths. Her gaze shifted to his slacks and the prominent bulge pressing against the front of his pants. Her face flamed with embarrassment. Lord, she had arched against him. . . . She had . . .

Her lower body felt unbearably empty. She wanted to run her finger up and down his length, to hold him without any clothes in the way. She wanted his skin against hers, his hardness filling her . . .

Mortified by her behavior and her feelings, she pushed herself upright. No one, she was glad to see, was looking at them. The other people were wrapped up either in the music or in the person beside them.

Her instincts urged her to run away and hide. "I'd like to go now."

"Wait." Jay sat up and grabbed her hand, preventing the quick escape to the car she had planned.

Knowing how red and swollen her lips must look, she rolled her lips inward in an effort to hide the evidence of his kisses.

"You never answered my question," he said gruffly, his gaze on her mouth, then on her desire-softened features.

"What question?" She could remember nothing but how, just a few moments before, she had craved him with every cell and nerve in her body.

"Do you like the way I taste?"

She gave a short, purely sarcastic laugh. "No, Jay. Not at all."

"*Tell me.*"

He wasn't going to let her off easily. Her gaze slid away from his. "Wasn't it obvious?"

"It was very nice, but I still want to hear you say it."

Nice? *Nice?* What had just happened between them had tilted her world, but he only regarded it as nice. *Damn* the man!

With a finger against the side of her chin, he turned her toward him. "Tell me."

She willed her clamoring nerves to stillness. "*Yes*, Jay," she said tightly, "I like the way you tasted. Are you satisfied?"

"Not even close."

Her heart gave a heavy thud. "Now that your ego has been stroked, can we please go?"

"It's not my ego that I'd like stroked right now," he drawled, "but yes, we can go."

Heat rose in her cheeks, and she scrambled to her feet.

The short drive home was accomplished in silence. As soon as Jay pulled his car into the driveway of his home, Emily reached for the door handle.

"Wait a minute." Jay switched off the car. "You're upset."

"No, really—"

"You're upset, and I owe you an apology."

The resignation in his voice caught her attention. He was accepting a responsibility that, as far as she was concerned, wasn't his. "No, you don't. You didn't force me to do a thing. It's my fault."

"Yours?"

She had wanted everything that happened, plus more, but there was no way she could say it aloud. Even the thought made her want to groan with embarrassment. "You've got nothing to apologize for. We simply got carried away, and I think it's better if we forget what happened, don't you?"

"Forgetting would be a neat trick," he said flatly. "I don't think I'm up to it."

"You're going to have to."

"Emily—"

She held up a hand. "I'm tired now. I'm going upstairs. Good night."

Emily undressed and slipped on an old T-shirt she had brought from her apartment. She was trembling, she realized, as she curled up in a big overstuffed chair by the window and gazed down at the garden.

Stupid. She felt so incredibly stupid. She had gotten lost in Jay's arms, and if it hadn't been for his cool head, they would have ended up making love right there in the park.

She couldn't believe it!

Except . . . She drew up her knees, wrapped her arms around her legs, and rocked back and forth. Deep inside she still ached for him. What was happening to her? Suddenly she was a mass of need and nerves. A man with leaf-green eyes and a touch like fire had come into her life and knocked all her supports out from under her. There were times when she felt as if she would come apart if he didn't make love to her.

But she *had* to get herself under control, because she also knew without a doubt that she would come apart if he did.

A knock sounded at the door; her whole body jerked.

"Emily, it's Jay."

His voice came to her through the door. Slowly she unfolded herself from the chair. Her legs felt so weak, she wasn't sure how long they would hold her upright. She closed her fingers around the doorknob, but her hand was shaking so much, she couldn't turn it. "What is it?" she asked instead.

"Would you please open the door?"

He sounded impatient, and she couldn't blame him. She was acting with all the composure of a teenager after her first kiss.

She opened the door without realizing she had done it. He was still dressed as he had been for the concert, but his face looked even harder than usual, his eyes darker. She supposed she should be afraid of him. She wasn't, though. All she could think of was that she would like to sink against him, absorb him with her senses and become a part of him. She was losing her mind.

Without moving to enter the room, he extended his hand toward her. "Here."

She gazed at him uncomprehendingly. "What?"

"The money. The five thousand dollars for the day."

The money. She had forgotten the money.

As the enormity of what had happened swept over her, she swayed and reached for the door to steady herself.

"Are you all right?" he asked with concern.

All right? She almost laughed. She had forgotten the reason, the *only* reason, why she was here with him! How could she have done that? The money was so important!

Jay. *He* was the reason she had forgotten, and she only had to look at him to know why. None of what she had been feeling had disappeared. Her body still throbbed for him, her eyes still hungrily drank him in.

With as much dignity as she could muster, she took the money from him. "Thank you."

"Emily—"

"I'd like to go to bed now. I'll see you in the morning. Good night." Not trusting herself to look at him again, she shut the door.

With a long and violent oath Jay turned on his heels and strode to his room. Once there, he stripped himself of his clothes and headed for the shower. Moments later cool water, turned up full force, beat down on him.

Emily had looked absolutely stricken when she had

seen the money, he thought grimly, leaning against the tiled wall. Dammit, how could he have foreseen that instead of diminishing in importance, the issue of the money would grow into a huge issue between them?

At the time it had seemed so simple to him. She obviously needed the money. He had it. He wanted her.

The offer had come right off the top of his head, and the instant he had made it, her reaction had told him he was on the right track, that this time she might not turn him down.

It had been in the way she looked at him, as if she couldn't believe what he was saying, but at the same time, as if she couldn't afford to dismiss him out of hand as she had done consistently for two straight weeks.

He didn't know why she needed money, only that she did. At first he hadn't given the matter much thought. The money meant very little to him, and if giving it to her would give him a chance with her, so much the better.

But now he tried to see the matter from her point of view and what he saw didn't make him happy. Distilled down to its essence, he had taken advantage of her need.

Tonight she had let herself go. Sweet heaven, she had been so willing and responsive. It had taken every particle of willpower he possessed to pull away from her. Despite the cool water pouring over him, he still burned for her. But when he had given her the money she hadn't even been able to look him in the eye.

And he knew why.

She couldn't allow herself to get close to a man who in effect had bought her.

Dammit, their time together was only just beginning, but if he didn't think of something quick, their ten days were going to come to an end, and he still wouldn't have what more and more he was coming to *need* instead of just want. *Emily*.

With a vicious turn of the faucet the cool water turned cold.

He closed his eyes, and a vision of Emily came into his head. Lovely, still, unknowingly sexy.

He wanted everything she had. Her intensity, her passion. . . . Dammit, he wanted her heart.

FIVE

Emily awoke before dawn, feeling uneasy, though she told herself she had no reason to feel that way. Despite what happened between her and Jay last night, she should be on top of the world today. After months of despair there was finally hope.

None of the doctors had been able to tell her how far her mother could progress, given the proper treatment. Now, with Jay's money, Emily would be assured that her mother would have every chance. And giving her that chance was the most important thing in the world to Emily.

So why was she feeling anxious? She glanced over at the dresser and her purse. The *money*.

She slid off the bed to her feet, hurried across the carpet, and grabbed her purse.

The money was still there. Ten thousand dollars.

She'd had to make sure. She was too used to the

sudden, the unexpected, the tragic, to take anything for granted.

Today she would pay Mrs. Thompson for two months, deposit several hundred into checking, and then put the rest in a safe-deposit box she planned to rent.

She stared down at the money. It and the additional amount Jay would give her represented a future for her mother, and for that she was extremely grateful.

Unfortunately the money also represented payment from Jay to her. Every time she thought about the arrangement between them, she had to fight the urge to be sick. She wanted the money, she needed the money, but she *hated* taking the money. The situation was perfectly ludicrous.

What must Jay think of her? They could put all kinds of names to what they were doing—arrangement, deal—but the reality was she had allowed him to buy her.

Longing swamped her. What would their relationship have been like, she wondered, if things had been different? What if being raised in an abusive household hadn't conditioned her to turn him down when he had first asked her out? Her rejection hadn't been anything against him personally—her habit was to turn all men down.

But what if she had been a happy, carefree young woman with no hang-ups or fears of commitment of any type and she'd been able to say yes that first day he had walked into the shop? What if they had gone on a regular date, maybe to a movie or out to dinner? Would he have asked her out again after their first date and would they still be dating? Would their relationship have been able to mature slowly into something deeper and richer?

She let out a long breath. In this instance speculation was a huge waste of time, because unfortunately none of the "what ifs" were true. Her fears and defenses had been formed a long time ago when she had been four years old. That was when she had first seen her stepfather hit her mother, then her mother forgive him in the name of love.

Because of it and many more scenes like it over the years, she was scared to death of a relationship, of giving herself up to a man, of falling totally, hopelessly in love.

As far as she was concerned, love for a man was the most dangerous emotion a woman could have.

She thought of Jay's gentleness, then impatiently shook her head. She didn't trust his gentleness. Jay was intrigued with her, that was all. She had turned him down—something he obviously wasn't used to—so he'd come up with an offer she couldn't refuse.

Then he had started his probing, trying to figure her out, as if she were some complicated puzzle. But she refused to tell him anything important about herself, anything that might reveal how scarred and frightened she was on the inside. So his intrigue with her had grown. She was sure if she thought about it long enough, she would be able to see and appreciate the irony.

She gazed at the door. Was he up? Throughout her body, nerves twisted like live electrical wires. After last night she was definitely edgy at the prospect of seeing him.

Yet, funnily enough, she also couldn't wait.

With a frown on her face she turned and headed for the shower, and a short time later, dressed in a pair of faded blue jeans and a gold T-shirt, she walked into the breakfast room.

"Good morning, Miss Stanton."

Emily stopped in her tracks at the sight of a tall, sturdy-looking woman wearing a tailored blue-linen tunic over black-linen slacks. Incongruently, large, glittery earrings dangled to her shoulders.

The woman's expression was warm and friendly. "I'm Roberta. What would you like for breakfast?"

"Anything you have will be fine," she said, walking slowly forward. "You must be John's wife."

"That's right, and you must be the young lady who's staying here with Mr. Barrett."

Emily couldn't prevent the blush that stained her cheeks. She had probably blushed more in the last few days than she had in her entire life, she thought ruefully. "Call me Emily, please."

"Glad to." Roberta held up a gleaming silver coffee-pot. "Would you like a cup?"

"Yes, thank you."

Roberta poured the coffee and handed it to her. "Sorry we haven't met before, but I've been busy in my kitchen, and besides"—she gave Emily a speculative glance—"I'm not used to Mr. Barrett having company."

"No?"

Roberta shook her head. "He's never even had a woman stay the night, at least I don't *think* he has. I've sure never seen any evidence of it. Course, there've been times when he hasn't come home until the next morning. I always figured he'd just rather stay at the woman's place than bring her back here."

Despite herself, Emily was fascinated by these revelations. "Really?"

Roberta nodded. "I think it's because he considers his home private. Can't tolerate strangers in it for more than a few hours at a time—like that party the other night." She crossed her arms beneath her ample bosom and gave Emily an eagle-eyed stare. "But then of course there's you. And the thing I can't get over is that he asked me to prepare a separate bedroom. . . ."

"Uh, yes, well, our relationship is sort of hard to explain."

"Are you related to him in some way?" she asked, her tone hopeful that the explanation would solve the mystery.

"No."

The other woman shook her head in puzzlement, sending the glittery earrings dancing. "A pretty thing like you not sharing his room. I just can't understand it, but don't mind me. I don't mean to be nosy. In fact John has told me in no uncertain terms that it's none of my business." She brightened. "But then John can be a real stick-in-the-mud. Fortunately I can always get him to loosen up and show his other side." Her smile broadened. "But then that's another story."

Emily's imagination faltered at what John's other side might be. She couldn't begin to envision John loosened up. She couldn't even imagine Roberta and him together, much less married.

Roberta seemed to recall her duties. Waving a hand toward the sideboard behind her, which was ladened with silver serving dishes, she said, "Help yourself to anything you like. Mr. Barrett has made it clear to me that this is to be considered your home while you're here, and he wants you to feel comfortable. Of course he probably told you not to go up to the third floor. That's off limits, even to me."

Still trying to imagine John loosening up, Emily was a little slow on the uptake. "Third floor?"

"Third floor," Roberta confirmed. "The attic. Now, if you need anything at all, you'll find me in the kitchen."

Just then Jay walked into the room. "Roberta, would you have John bring my car around, please."

Both women turned to look at him.

"You're going somewhere?" Emily felt dumb for stating the obvious, but she was surprised. He had waited for her at the house yesterday afternoon while she had been gone, and she had simply assumed he would do the same today. In fact, she realized, she found a certain amount of comfort in the thought.

At the sideboard he poured himself a cup of coffee. "I'm going in to work for a little while."

"Why? I thought you'd taken time off."

Instead of answering her, he glanced at the older woman hovering by the door that led to the kitchen. "Thank you, Roberta. Great earrings, by the way."

Roberta beamed at the compliment. "Thanks. I'll tell John about the car right away."

As soon as Roberta had disappeared into the kitchen, Jay turned to Emily, and his gaze swept over her, registering in seconds everything about her. "Something's come up at the office. Since you said you wouldn't be here today, I thought I'd go in."

"I see." To her astonishment she heard disappointment in her voice. Why on earth would she be disappointed that he was letting his real life infringe on what was supposed to be their time? It annoyed her that she had even thought of the question. It especially annoyed her that she didn't have an answer.

Jay's brow rose. "Unless you'll change your plans?"

She shook her head. "I can't."

"Are you sure? Give me a reason, and I'll stay."

The surface of her skin warmed at the slight huskiness of his voice. "I'm sure."

He put his cup down, walked to her, and curled

his long fingers around her upper arms, just below the T-shirt sleeves so that he could feel her bare skin. "My original plan doesn't seem to be working out, does it?"

"I'm not worried about it," she said more stiffly than she had intended. "It's just that you're paying me an awful lot of money, and I'm concerned that you feel you get your money's worth."

His eyes narrowed. "I told you last night, forget the money."

"It's a little hard."

His thumbs moved up and down over the sensitive skin of her inner arms, caressing. "I realize that, but I'm not sure this is going to work if you don't."

It *had* to work, she thought. Despite her confused feelings about him and the growing need she felt for him, it had to work. "You're right. I'll try."

"I'd feel so much better if I thought you were trying because you wanted to be with me instead of because you wanted the money."

The memory of how last night she had completely forgotten the money put a hard edge in her voice. "As I recall, wanting to be with you wasn't part of the deal."

He abruptly released her. "What time do you think you'll be back?"

"I'm not sure. Sometime this afternoon."

"I'll try to be back by then." She nodded, staring at one of his shirt buttons.

With a muffled curse, he caught her chin and tilted her head up. "It's going to get better. I promise."

She shrugged. "I told you—I'm only worried about you."

"Then stop. Having you here in the house is making me very happy."

"I don't see how—"

He claimed her lips with a kiss that might have taken place only seconds after the last one he had given her the night before. It was like a continuation of the passion that had exploded between them at the concert. The kiss was deep and fiery, and she felt it all the way down to her toes. As was the case at the concert, she could muster no resistance to him. She liked his mouth on hers, she reveled in the feel of his tongue against hers, she loved the way he molded her against him, fitting the length of her body against his hard contours. And all of those things were why she was grateful that he kept the kiss short.

He drew his head back, and his eyes glinted dark green. "It just makes me happy," he said quietly, "that's all."

The transfer to the new nursing home was physically hard on her mother, but it went smoothly. Elizabeth Horton turned out to be very nice. Though in a wheelchair, she was a commanding figure, giving rapid-fire orders to the attendants, cautioning them to take care in the handling of her obviously more incapacitated new roommate, and ordering an attendant to bring more pillows and a pot of hot tea. In a gentler voice she fussed over Emily's mother, asking her opinion on where she wanted things, making sure everything was to her satisfaction.

Elizabeth would be good for her mother, Emily concluded.

When everyone had left and Elizabeth had wheeled herself out of the room to check on the tea, Emily drew up a chair beside the bed and took her mother's hand. "So what do you think, Mom? Isn't it nice here?"

Her mother smiled tiredly. "Very."

"I've already spoken with Mrs. Thompson. Tomorrow a doctor and a physical therapist will give you an evaluation, and then you'll be started on a program."

"I'm looking forward to it. I feel so useless like I am now."

Her mother's sad tone went straight to Emily's heart. "You're going to get better. I just know it." She squeezed her mother's hand and felt its frailty. "Do you remember that I told you I won't be able to come by to see you for about a week?" Her mother nodded, but her eyes were slowly closing, and Emily realized she'd soon be asleep. "Mom, listen to me for just a minute longer. I know you're going to be busy during the next week, but I want you to think about something. I want you to think about divorcing Ralph."

"You know I can't do that," her mother said softly, the words slightly slurred.

"Mom, I realize you were raised to believe that once you were married, it was forever, but that man has made your life a hell on earth. You're away from him now, and if I have anything to say about it, you'll never go back to him. Once you're better, you and I can have a good life here in Dallas."

There was no reply, and Emily realized that her mother had fallen asleep. Tears came to her eyes as she looked down at her. "I've got to get that man out of your life once and for all," she whispered. "When are you going to listen to me?"

Emily's mood lightened as she drove back to Jay's house. In a couple of months when her mother was stronger, she would renew her efforts to get her mother to divorce her stepfather. She would never give up on that. And for now her mother was safe.

Tonight when she went to sleep, she wouldn't have to worry whether this was the night Ralph would finally kill her mother. And for the first time in a long while she didn't have to worry whether she was getting the proper care. For months she had felt as if she were carrying around a heavy load on her shoulders. Now she was actually beginning to feel lighter, almost as if she had lost a drastic amount of weight.

When she arrived back at the house, John informed her that Jay hadn't returned from the office yet. Trying to convince herself she wasn't disappointed, she went to her room to freshen up. On impulse and without giving herself time to think about her reasons, she changed out of her jeans and T-shirt and into something else that was hers, a blue-flowered cotton sundress with a scoop neck and tiny straps that formed an X across her bare back.

Leaving her room, she cast a glance toward the double doors a few feet away. Again on impulse she decided to explore.

Jay's bedroom was much as she had imagined it would be, large, luxuriously furnished, infinitely comfortable, and utterly serene. In fact his immense bed reminded her of a cloud, with its white-colored padded headboard, plump down comforter, and endless mounds of pillows.

The more she saw of Jay's house, the more it appealed to her. Like its owner, it was seductive. Within its walls one really could shut out the world.

She stared at his bed, imagining him lying there. What would it be like to be made love to on a cloud? By Jay?

She momentarily lingered by the sculpted bust of a little girl with her nose buried in a flower. The piece had obviously been done by the same person who had done the sculpture of the little boy. Even though the figure of the little girl was cast in bronze, there was a sense of warmth about her, a sense of wonder.

Jay obviously liked children, she reflected, but then that was natural. A man like him would want children of his own—sons and daughters to love and spoil and raise to go, perhaps, one day, into his business. And of course children would require a mother, which would mean he would require a wife. . . .

In a pensive, less lighthearted mood, she left his room and headed for the stairs, but the sight of another stairway caught her attention and brought her to a stop. It was a narrow stairway leading up to the third floor—the attic, she supposed. Roberta had said Jay didn't allow her up there. What could he possibly have up there that he didn't want anyone to see?

The temptation to go up and investigate was almost more than she could stand. Fortunately in the end good sense prevailed. She didn't want to know what was up there, she told herself. When the time limit on their agreement ran out, she would be better off parting from Jay as strangers. Strangers who had the ability to block out everything around them while they kissed and strained against each other. . . .

John was crossing the hall as she made her way down the stairs. Catching sight of her, he came to a stop and waited for her. "Mr. Barrett is in his study, Miss Stanton."

"He's back?" She glanced at her watch. Heavens, she had been upstairs longer than she had thought. "Thank you, John."

She found Jay leaning back in his chair, his feet up on the desk. "Hi. How long have you been back?"

"Not long."

She glanced around and saw that a panel of the wall had been opened and a sophisticated computer system sat in the recess. The computer was on, but its screen was blank. "I didn't know that was there."

"I designed it so that no one would be able to tell what was behind it."

"Are you working?"

He smiled. "Just thinking." Lowering his feet to the floor, he held out his hand to her, and she walked around the desk. When she reached him, he pulled her down onto his lap.

At first her spine remained ramrod straight, but when his hand sought and found the bare skin of her back and slipped his fingers beneath the straps, she felt the stiffness begin to melt out of her.

"I like your dress," he said huskily, smoothing his palm up and down her spine.

"Thank you. It's old."

"I still like it, and you look beautiful and sexier than hell in it."

Warmth invaded her lower limbs, and involuntarily she softened, leaning against his chest, sliding her arm around his neck.

He pressed his lips to her ear and whispered. "So, is whatever you've had to do these last two days done?"

"Yes," she said, wondering if she would ever understand how he could have such a powerful effect on her.

His teeth fastened on the lobe of her ear and gently nibbled. "Does that mean that you're all mine now?"

A feathery sensation shuddered up her spine. "My *time* is."

With a smile he pulled his head back. "So cautious."

"Yes," she admitted, lifting a finger to trace the curve of his bottom lip. He smiled at her so easily. Surely such an easy smile couldn't be trusted. "I've found it's the best way."

With a hand behind her head he drew her mouth to his for a brief, light kiss. "With me you don't have to be cautious." He kept his lips on hers so that they brushed over hers as he spoke.

Heat crawled through her veins. "With you most of all, I think. Look at me. I'm sitting on your lap, for goodness' sake. You held out your hand, and I came to you without really knowing why I was doing it."

He laughed, and his breath fanned over her mouth. "Maybe you did it because it feels good to be held and kissed and stroked."

There was no way she could argue with him, not when she practically purred like a kitten at his every touch or almost cried out in protest every time he ended a kiss. She was like someone who had been on a strict diet all her life and now she was suddenly being fed all sorts of treats. She was very much afraid they both knew that if it wasn't for his control, she would have ended up on her back days ago with her legs spread, urging him into her. The mere thought caused a fire to flare up in her. She straightened away from him.

He regarded her with a steady gaze, but made no comment on her action. "Now that you're finished with whatever it was that took you away from me yesterday and today, are you going to tell me what you were doing?"

"You weren't here today," she said, feeling the need to set the record straight and put part of the blame on him.

"I would have been if you had."

She couldn't find a false note in his flatly stated sentence. "No," she said softly. "I'm not going to tell you."

"Tell me at least one thing. Does it involve another man?"

"I told you—"

"No, yesterday I asked you if the reason you were smiling was because of a man. This is a different question."

She shook her head. "No, Jay. I wouldn't have accepted your offer if there'd been another man, at least one in the way you mean." Intent on depriving him of a chance to probe further, she slipped from his lap and put some distance between them. Waving her hand toward the computer system, she asked, "Are you working on a problem?"

"A *potential* problem."

"Potential?"

He chuckled. "The truth is, there are rumors floating around in the industry that trouble may be just over the horizon for me, but there's no way to know yet. I've decided not to worry about it until I know more."

Nine out of ten rumors in his business never became a fact. He had a feeling, though, this one would. Unfortunately until it did, he wouldn't know what weapon was being used against him.

She gazed at him thoughtfully, trying to imagine a problem severe enough to concern him. To her he seemed invulnerable. He was head of a telecommunications conglomerate he had founded, and if the occasional articles she scanned in the newspapers about it were true, his business was more than thriving, it was growing. "Could the problem be serious?"

"Maybe. Only time will tell."

"I once read an article about you in the newspaper, and it said you started your company with ideas and products that you designed. Are you a designer or a businessman?"

"My education is in engineering, but over the years I've discovered an aptitude for business. For the most part now I leave the designing to others. I have one of the best research-and-development companies in the industry."

The information only confirmed what she had already known. Jay was an extraordinary man. He probably would have been good at anything he tried.

"Is there anything else you'd like to know?"

She shook her head. "No. I was simply curious, that's all."

"Ask me anything, anytime. In the meantime, is there anything special you'd like to do tonight?"

The question sent her on a meandering course around the room. What could they do, she wondered, that wouldn't end with her losing her head and almost making love to him? "We could go to a movie." At least in a movie theater they'd be sitting upright with other people around them, not reclining on a quilt, as they had been last night, with no one behind them to see what they were doing.

"If that's what you'd like to do."

"Or we could go to dinner." That might be better, she thought. A restaurant would be well lit, not dark like a movie house or with only distant lights to illuminate their lovemaking as the park had been.

"We could do both."

"Or we could go to an art gallery." *Better yet*, she thought. They'd be standing *and* walking in a lighted place, surrounded by other people.

"I know of a couple of galleries we could go to."

"Or we could stay here and watch TV." They would be alone, and the room would probably be dark, but for some reason the idea appealed to her. Maybe because she couldn't remember the last time she had watched TV. She was usually too tired.

"We can do any or all of those things if you like." She seemed more relaxed, he thought, which made him happy. But she was still as closed as ever. He sighed, realizing his head hurt.

Emily stopped in front of the Monet and gazed up at it. "I bet your garden would look like this after a rain."

"Maybe. In a certain season and in a certain light."

She turned to look at him. "You know what I find strange? You have valuable works of art like this one all through the house, but I haven't seen a single family picture. None of friends either."

His lips quirked. "You should talk. Your apartment wasn't exactly overflowing with family memorabilia."

"At least I have *one* picture." She paused as she thought of the third floor. "Unless you keep the pictures someplace I haven't been."

He rubbed his temple. "No, I don't. I never had a family. My mother died when I was very young, and my father took off soon afterward. If there were ever any pictures, they disappeared a long time ago."

"Who raised you?"

"More sets of foster parents than I can or want to remember."

She had asked enough, she told herself firmly, but then frowned as she watched him rub his temple. "Do you have a headache?"

He dropped his hand away from his head. "A little one."

"There's no such thing as a little headache. They're all bad." She hesitated, then went to him. "Let me see if I can help."

He looked at her in surprise. "How?"

She walked around behind him and reached over the

back of the chair to his head. The chair's high back put her arms at an awkward angle, but she made an attempt, slowly circling her fingers on his temples. "I'm good at massage. My mother used to get headaches all the time, and this would help her."

"Why would your mother get headaches?"

"Tension," she replied absently. She repositioned herself and stood on tiptoes, but the angle remained awkward.

"Does she get them anymore?"

"Sometimes." It was just that she had so many other health problems now, her headaches seemed minor. She thought of her mother in the sunny, airy room at the new nursing home with the formidable Elizabeth fussing over her and smiled.

"This feels wonderful," he murmured.

Giving an abrupt exclamation, she walked around to the front of the chair and sat down on his lap. "The angle wasn't right. Maybe I can do it better this way." She lifted her fingers back to his temples.

"If it will get you in my lap, remind me to get a headache more often."

He didn't need a headache, she thought sourly. He only had to beckon. Glancing down at him, she saw that his eyes were half closed. "Is it feeling better yet?"

His brow creased against the pain. "Not really."

"Close your eyes. This will work if you can just relax."

That would be hard, he thought, with her sitting on

his lap, the side of her breast brushing against his chest and her fragrance wrapping around him like a silk ribbon of enticing femininity. He glanced at her through his lowered lashes and saw the concentration on her face as her fingers moved from his temples into his hair.

"You have magic fingers," he said softly, and began to imagine how they would feel on the rest of his body.

"Mmm?" Distracted by the heat and smell of him, she got up and sat back down again, this time astride him, with her legs on either side of his.

"I'm sorry," she said when she saw his eyes shoot open, "but this is the only way I can really do it right."

"By all means do it right."

His words barely registered. She was beginning to wonder if she had unconsciously taken advantage of his headache so that she could be close to him and put her hands on him without seeming sexually needy. Was she really that hopeless? Lord, she prayed it wasn't true.

She delved her fingers through his hair and began to touch pressure points on his head. At first he flinched because the spots were sore, but she continued, and the soreness eased away. Or maybe he didn't notice it as much, because his body and his mind were riveted on her.

"Relax," she murmured.

Impossible, he thought. His pain had changed from a throbbing in his head to one in his groin. He could feel himself hardening as the blood surged to his lower body.

He put his hands on her waist and flexed his fingers. If he didn't have her soon, he thought, his frustration was going to boil over, and he had no idea what would happen then. He had never had his control tested this way before, had never wanted to this extent.

Heat was gathering in every part of her body, her bones were in danger of melting, and she was going to give herself away if she couldn't get her mind to think of something else. "You haven't had an easy life, have you?"

He should pay attention to what she was saying, he thought vaguely. It was one of the first times she had asked him a personal question. "Why do you think that?"

She shrugged. "I don't know. Just an impression I have." His scalp was a lot less tight since she had started the massage, she reflected with satisfaction. But the cost to her was that her insides were coiled with heat. She had been telling herself that she'd chosen her position because it was the only way she knew how to do the massage effectively. The problem was, she didn't believe herself. She had the awful feeling that she had deliberately placed herself over him so that she could feel the rigid thickness of his sexual need beneath her. And it felt wonderful.

"Have you?" she asked again in hopes it would get both their minds off of what was happening to them physically.

At her waist his fingers flexed again. "Does anyone?"

She gave a shaky laugh. "Someone must, or else life wouldn't make any sense."

His hands slid down to her hips. "Does that mean you didn't?"

She felt as if pure, unadulterated desire had replaced the blood in her veins. "We were talking about you." She was growing hotter by the minute. Desperate for some relief, she shifted slightly, then realized what she had done. The soft, sensitive folds of her femininity were centered over him exactly.

Her fingers stilled in his hair and she looked down into his eyes. The hunger and fire there stole her breath away.

Without a word he tightened his hands on her waist, and he began moving her on him.

Pleasure surged through her like none she'd ever known before. Without realizing it, she let her hands drop from his head to his shoulders.

"You got rid of my headache," he said thickly. "But now I've got an ache of a different kind." Leaning forward he pressed his mouth against her neck, gripped her hips, and rocked her on him.

Tension circled through her, growing, increasing, making her frantic. A whole new world of sensations was opening up inside her, a world that both frightened and enticed her. She dug her fingers into his shoulders, holding on.

"I'm going to enjoy the hell out of watching that innocence of yours turn into wonder," he whispered in a rasp.

She wasn't sure what he was saying. A curtain of heat had descended around her and was rapidly closing her off from reality. Pain of unfulfillment gripped her. He knew how to help her, but she wasn't sure she could allow him to. She wanted him, but . . .

Seconds, minutes, she wasn't sure how much time passed, but suddenly she realized he had stilled beneath her and was no longer moving her. And when she did realize it, she had to bite her bottom lip to stop from crying out.

"You said no," Jay told her. The words might have contained barbed wire for all the pain they caused him. He was having to fight against a savage need to forget his morals and to say to hell with his resolves. And the line between winning and losing in this battle was nearly nonexistent.

"I did?" She hadn't even heard herself.

"Whenever you say no, Emily, I'll stop. You have to want me more than you want to breathe."

The thing was, she couldn't breathe now for all the heat in her chest. She couldn't draw any fresh air into her lungs. She was burning with a fire that was consuming all her oxygen. Soon she was afraid breathing would no longer be an option, and then it wouldn't matter what she wanted.

SIX

The next few days passed too slowly for Emily, and in an odd way too quickly. She was with Jay almost constantly. They did all the things she had suggested and more. They sat in a darkened theater, watching a movie and sharing popcorn. Afterward she found herself unable to remember what she had seen, only that Jay had held her hand and put his arm around her.

They went to art galleries, where they spent hours exchanging thoughts on the pieces they saw. Mostly they agreed with each other, but every once in a while they got into a lighthearted disagreement, and when they did, Jay invariably started laughing. And the deep, husky, infectious sound always made her forget what she had been saying.

One night they stayed home and watched television. They had dinner on TV trays and ended up lying on the couch in each other's arms.

In fact no matter what they did, he rarely let her get beyond his reach. He kissed and touched her constantly, but he always stopped just short of actually making love. She told herself she was exceedingly grateful for his control, but alarmingly she couldn't always convince herself. A very large part of her was so frustrated that at times she was sure her sanity was in danger.

Time after time he brought her to the point where she was moments away from begging him to make love to her. Yet he always maintained the presence of mind to pull away before she did.

More and more she resented his control, just as she resented the way he could make sweetness burn through her veins until there was no thought, only feeling. She resented it because he was the one who always stopped, proving to her that he had a more powerful effect on her than she did on him.

The money.

She had come to rue her request that he give it to her at the end of each day.

She was taking the money to help her mother, not for herself. But Jay didn't know that. And even if he did, her reason wouldn't make any difference to him. She was just another thing he was trying to buy. And ultimately, she told herself, it shouldn't matter to her what he thought of her. It shouldn't, but it did.

"You're not eating."

Emily looked up at Jay. They were having a late

lunch in the garden. It was a warm day, and she could hear birds singing in a nearby tree. There was a sense of permanence and security about the garden with its weathered brick walls, trees that looked to be at least half a century old or more, and well-trodden walkways that meandered among the flowers. But she wouldn't be surprised to find that the brick wall and walkways had been built and the trees planted since Jay had moved in. He had a way of putting his fingerprints all over his possessions. So much so that she was beginning to wonder if it was only a matter of time before his fingerprints covered her completely.

"I'm not hungry."

"You haven't had much of an appetite these last few days."

"You're mistaken. I've eaten more than enough."

Jay frowned. There was a strain between them that, instead of getting better as the days passed, was getting worse. Practically the only time he could make her forget her self-consciousness was when he was kissing her. But if he could see signs of tension in her, he could *feel* the tension in himself.

He couldn't seem to prevent himself from taking her into his arms. But each time he had to let her go, he felt as if he was tearing off a piece of himself. Any time now his control was going to blow wide open, and when that happened, he wasn't going to be able to stop himself from ripping off her clothes and making love to her until they were both exhausted. He was experienced enough to know that she wouldn't say no to him, that in fact she would urge him on. And the knowledge worked on his mind and body, making him crazy.

But he also knew that after the lovemaking she would hate him. And that made it unacceptable.

He wasn't sure what to do. He wasn't a man who admitted defeat easily. He always felt there was one more thing he could do, one more thing he could say. And in this case he wasn't near ready to give up.

John appeared at his side and handed him a folded piece of paper.

He took the note and scanned it. "Thank you, John." With a grimace he looked at Emily. "This note is a reminder from a business associate of mine. He and his wife are heading up a charity function tonight, and they're expecting me to attend."

"And you don't want to?"

"Not particularly, but it's a commitment I did make. . . . The question is will you come with me? I won't go unless you do."

"Thank you, Jay," she said dryly. "Nothing like putting the entire responsibility on me."

"That's not my intention. I simply want you to enjoy yourself. If you don't want to go, we'll do something else."

She sighed. "I don't really care. It's no big deal. I don't mind going."

"And you'll stay beside me this time?"

She saw the twinkle in his eyes and responded in kind. "Well, I wouldn't go quite *that* far."

He smiled, pleased at her teasing tone. In some ways at least she felt more comfortable with him now. "How far will you go? As far as wearing the jade silk dress that I bought for you?"

Her eyes narrowed. She had worn the gold dress to his party, but since then hadn't worn any of the clothes he had bought for her. After several moments' consideration she relented. "Why not? I have to wear something, and I don't think my jeans would be right for the occasion."

He tilted his head to one side and regarded her thoughtfully. "You know, I really like you in this agreeable mood."

"I've been nothing *but* agreeable, Jay." Too agreeable at times, she thought, thinking of how easily she turned to fire in his arms.

Deliberately forcing her gaze away from him, she found herself looking at the back of the house. It was a wonderful place, and its owner equally wonderful in his own way. But the fact remained, neither could ever be hers, and as long as she remembered it, she would be fine.

With his seductive powers he had lured her into his life and into his home. True, she had grown rather used to being with him. But when their time came to part, she would be able to walk away whole. She was counting on that ability with everything that was in her.

She pointed toward the attic. "Roberta told me that the third floor is off-limits."

"Did she?"

"She said it was even off-limits to her."

"It's just that I don't like her or most people up there."

"Why not?"

He chuckled. "You sound so suspicious. What is it, Emily? Do you think I have a crazy wife hidden away up there like Mr. Rochester in *Jane Eyre*?"

"If that were the case, you'd have to have her meals catered." She shrugged. "Either that or you're starving the poor lady to death."

His lips twitched. "I can tell you've given the matter a great deal of thought."

"Not really."

"Uh-huh. Right. What if I told you there's nothing at all sinister or even mildly suspect up there?"

"Then I'd ask why you keep people out."

"Because I consider the third floor my own private space."

"The entire *house* is your own private space, Jay."

"Then let me put it this way: The things I do up there are very personal to me." He paused and gave her a measuring look. "But don't take my word for it. Go up and see for yourself."

Her mouth dropped open. "You'd let *me* up there?"

He shrugged. "Sure. In fact I'll take you right now if you want."

Her curiosity level rose. "Do you have to be with me when I go? I mean, do you have something up there you're afraid I'll steal?"

He laughed out loud. "No, Emily. I hate to disappoint that vivid imagination of yours, but I don't have a treasure trove hidden away. In fact if you see anything you want, you can have it."

Her curiosity was nearly overwhelming now. She had the greatest urge to rush to the third floor immediately to investigate. But one thing held her back. He had said that what was up there was very personal to him. At this point, with only a few days remaining on their deal, she didn't want to know more than she already did about him. In her mind, knowledge equaled a far higher level of intimacy than physical intimacy. And that kind of intimacy equaled lunacy.

"No, thank you," she said politely and stood. "Since we're going out tonight, I'd like to lie down for about an hour."

He frowned. "Are you tired?"

"A little." In fact she hadn't been sleeping well lately. Each night she found herself waking every few hours from dreams that, even though she couldn't remember their content, left her extremely unsettled. As a result she had been spending a great deal of time between midnight and dawn by her bedroom window, viewing the garden in ever-shifting light as the moon passed across the sky.

*   *   *

The party was being given at one of the city's newer luxury hotels and was in full swing when they arrived. Jay kept Emily's hand in his as he threaded his way through the crowd. Although Emily had not had the opportunity to attend many social functions, she wasn't particularly intimidated by them. In the various jobs she had held since she had been on her own, she had had no problem dealing with a cross section of people. Still, it made her feel good to have him holding her hand.

Jay stopped in front of an older couple. "Margie and Lionel, I'd like you to meet Emily Stanton. Emily, this is Margie and Lionel Thornton, our host and hostess for this evening."

Emily recognized the couple from Jay's party. "Hello," she said pleasantly. "Everything looks as if it's going wonderfully."

Margie, a middle-aged blond with soft features and flawless pink skin, rolled her eyes. "Thanks. I'm keeping my fingers crossed."

Lionel, a tall, robust man with a thick Texas drawl, clapped Jay on the back. "Glad to see you here tonight. Did you get my note? I was afraid you were going to give our little shindig a miss."

"That's exactly what I was going to do, even after I got your note." He put an arm around Emily and drew her against his side. "Fortunately for you, Emily said she'd come with me."

Margie smiled at her. "Thank you, Emily. We know Jay doesn't like these sorts of things, but it means a lot to have a man of his reputation and stature attend. It lends an event like this credibility."

Jay bent his head to Emily and said in a mock aside, "What she really means is they feel if they can get me to come, they can get anyone. And besides, they like the size of my checkbook."

Lionel nodded cheerfully. "That's about it."

A series of flashbulbs went off to Emily's right. She turned and saw a young man taking pictures across the room. He was the society photographer for the Dallas paper, she guessed, and made a mental note to avoid him.

"How did you two meet?" Margie asked.

It was a perfectly natural question, but Emily couldn't stop herself from stiffening at the question. Then she mentally scolded herself. She was being way too sensitive. It didn't matter that Margie thought she and Jay were here on a normal date. Margie had no way of knowing that she wouldn't be here unless he had bought her time, and even if she did know, it simply didn't matter. So then why, Emily wondered, did she feel so bad about it?

Jay waited for Emily to say something, and when she didn't, he spoke up. "I met Emily at the florist shop where she works. She has a very special gift for arranging flowers."

Emily glanced up at him, wondering why their meeting sounded so normal. When she thought of it, she remembered a jolting experience. And to her mind the money added a particularly abnormal twist.

"Really?" Margie asked with interest. "How wonderful. I wish I had known that. I could have used some advice on the arrangements for tonight."

"It looks to me as if you did fine. They're all lovely."

"Thank you, but I really couldn't decide on a theme. In fact, trying to come up with a fantastic theme that hadn't been used before drove me so crazy, I finally decided that our theme tonight would be *no* theme."

Emily saw another series of flashes go off, these closer to them. She glanced up at Jay. "If you wouldn't mind, I'd like to take a walk around and admire Margie's decorations."

He smiled down at her. "Your wish is my command."

Her heart fluttered. Damn the man. He looked absolutely spectacular tonight in his dark evening suit and white shirt.

"Lucky girl!" Margie said. "If I were you, Emily, I would come up with a whole list of wishes while he's still in this mood."

Lionel gave a hearty laugh. "And if I were you, Jay, I'd take those words back before it's too late."

"I'm afraid it was too late the moment I looked into those amber eyes of hers," Jay said.

His tone sounded embarrassingly intimate to Emily. She heard Margie and Lionel laugh. More flashbulbs, these even closer. "My wish is that you and I dance immediately," she said to him.

"What is the policy on wish changes?" Lionel asked jokingly.

Margie poked him in the arm. "It's a woman's prerogative to change her mind."

"I didn't change my mind," she said, staring up at Jay with a pleading look in her eye. "I still want to see the decorations, but first I want to dance."

"Then by all means." He took her hand. "Margie, Lionel, we'll see you later."

"Have fun," they chorused.

In the next room, where an orchestra played, Jay drew her into his arms. "What was wrong back there?"

"Nothing."

"They didn't say anything to upset you?" he asked, eyeing her intently.

"No, not at all. They were very nice. I simply wanted to dance."

"Well, then, who am I to complain?" He drew her closer against him. "I'll take any excuse to hold you."

She glanced around the room, and when she didn't see any sign of the photographer, she gave an inner sigh of relief. Since Jay hadn't had a photographer at his party, it hadn't occurred to her that one would be here. She needed to stay on the alert. It might not matter one way or the other if her picture was taken, but she couldn't afford to take any chances. Distracted, she stepped on Jay's foot. "Sorry. I haven't danced in a long time."

"Don't worry. Just relax and follow my lead."

There was no way she could relax, not pressed against his hard body as she was, not with his hand at her waist, his fingers moving restlessly. She was having trouble thinking, hearing. . . .

"What kind of music are they playing?" she asked, hoping conversation would get her mind off the now-familiar heat that had begun to build in her.

"Homogenized," he murmured, his mouth near her ear. "These orchestras that play on the society circuit take perfectly good songs and mellow them out until they sound like homogenized milk."

His breath warmed her ear, and his voice was soft and deep. "Shouldn't something *taste* like homogenized milk and a song *sound* like whatever?"

"Did you understand what I meant?"

"Yes, I guess I did."

"Then a song can sound like homogenized milk." He curled her hand inward until it was resting against his chest and rubbed his thumb across the back of her fingers. "You look incredibly beautiful tonight. Did you know that when you wear the color jade, tiny flecks of green show up in your eyes?"

She gave a shaky laugh and looked up at him. "You're making that up."

"Not even a little bit. You should wear jade more often."

The music changed to a new tune and slowed. His thighs moved against hers, his hard pelvis pressed, making her all too aware of his desire. Dangerously his desire matched exactly what she was feeling inside. "Maybe I will when I can afford to buy something."

"Is that your way of reminding me that you're not going to take any of the things I've bought for you when you leave?"

She wasn't sure. She was not only losing track of the conversation, but also of time and place. Her body was pulsating, not to the music, but to the rhythm of Jay's body. She was sure she could feel each beat of his heart, the swift flow of his blood, the pulsing throb of his desire. . . .

"I have to tell you I wish you wouldn't."

"What?" she asked blankly, looking up at him, and found herself staring at his beautifully shaped mouth. Her stomach clenched, and she was flooded with memories of all the times he had kissed her and turned her inside out with desire.

"Leave."

Everything was suddenly too much for her. She dropped her head to his shoulder, resting her face against the smooth fabric of his jacket and inhaling his scent into her system, where she was sure it would remain a part of her for all time. "Let's don't get into it, okay?"

We're going to have to soon," he said, his voice a deep, rumble in his chest. "I want you to stay with me, Emily. More money won't be a problem—"

She felt as if she had been doused with a pitcher of ice water. She shoved away from him, freeing herself, then stood there, appallingly unable to do anything but tremble. "Can we please get out of here?"

"What's wrong?"

"I want to go back to your house, that's what's wrong. And I'd like to be in a position to tell you exactly what you could do with your money, *that's* what's wrong. Now, are you going to take me or am I going to call a cab?"

His jaw tightened. "Let's go."

The atmosphere inside the car on the drive home was charged with a silence that grew thicker and more impenetrable as the minutes ticked by. When Jay pulled the car to a stop in the driveway, Emily got out as fast as she could. Everything in her was focused on getting as far away from him as possible.

She raced up the walkway, but when she got to the front door, she almost screamed. She had two choices, she realized. Ring the doorbell for John or wait for Jay to unlock the door with his key. She glanced over her shoulder and saw Jay strolling up the walk, his keys in his hand, his gaze steady and intent on her.

"You want to tell me what happened back there?"

She crossed her arms beneath her breasts. "What I want is to go upstairs and go to sleep."

He slipped the keys into his pocket and braced his arm against the door behind her, trapping her in a pocket of space heated and defined by his body. "Sorry, but I'm not ready to let you go."

"Does it matter at all what I want?"

"Listen to me, Emily," he said, taking her face in his free hand. "I realize you feel awkward about our arrangement. I thought time would help. I still think it might. But there's got to be something else . . . something I can do to make you feel more content here with me and more relaxed. Tell me and I'll do it. I want you to be happy."

Tears sprang to her eyes. Something must be terribly wrong with her, she thought. Jay was a man who could make her heart race and her blood sing and he was asking her what he could do to make her happy. Unfortunately she had never felt more miserable in her life.

"There's nothing," she whispered, blinking the tears away. "Just let me go upstairs."

"I'm not ready to let you go," he said, his words deliberately spaced, his voice almost a growl. "I can't."

"You're going to have to, Jay, because I don't think I can take this much longer."

* * *

She hadn't been in her room but a few minutes when she heard the knock on her door. Her heart sank. The damned money. What an irony both to need the money badly and to hate it with all her heart.

And now she was going to have to face Jay one more time tonight to take today's packet of five thousand dollars from him. It made her feel exceptionally cheap, but then again, she thought, desperately reaching for humor even if it was black, getting paid five thousand dollars a day put her in an extremely high-priced category. If it wasn't for her mother . . . but, no, there *was* her mother. Bracing herself, she went to answer the door.

"Here," he said, handing her several packets of money. "This is the rest of the money."

"The rest?" A glance showed her that she was holding twenty thousand dollars. "I don't understand. Why are you giving it to me now? We have three more days to go on our deal."

"Because I'm sick and tired of the money being between us. As of this moment I'm declaring our agreement null and void. I'm letting you out of the deal, Emily."

"You're—?" She glanced again at the money. "But you're still paying me for the next three days?"

"Yes."

"I don't understand," she said for the second time.

"It's simple. Consider yourself paid in full. You're free to do whatever you want. You can stay, or you can leave right now."

Stunned, she gazed up at him. Telling her she could leave was the last thing she had expected. "If you're ending the deal, it must mean you've changed your mind about me."

"You're not listening to what I'm saying, Emily. I thought the money would give me what I wanted, time with you."

"It did."

"Not in the way I wanted." He shoved his fingers through his hair. "Almost from the first minute I saw you, I wanted you, totally and completely, but you've always managed to keep part of yourself away from me."

"If you're talking about sex—"

"I am, and a hell of a lot more."

"But *you're* the one who always pulls back."

He reached for her upper arms and jerked her against his body. The contact burned her to her toes.

"Do you think I've been just *playing* with you?" he asked fiercely. "Do you think I've enjoyed touching you and kissing you until I'm ready to explode if I don't have you?"

"But—"

"I touch and kiss you, Emily, because when you're near, I can't do anything else. I *have* to." His voice was grindingly harsh, his expression stone hard, and his eyes glittered dark and forbidding. "The truth is, I want you more than ever. My gut is in a constant knot of need. I'm in *agony*, Emily. It's gotten to the point that I don't know how much longer I'll be able to control anything about our situation." He stopped and drew in a ragged breath. "But I don't want to take you and then have you wake up the next morning and hate me. *Remember?* I want you to want me more than you want to breathe, and that's the way it's got to be." He released her. "So here I am, Emily, waiting to hear what it is you want."

She wasn't sure she could speak. Emotion seemed to be clogging her throat. "What I want hasn't changed. I want the money."

"Then you'll be leaving."

His voice sounded flat and dull, but she couldn't be sure, because she also heard screaming, and it seemed to be coming from inside her mind. What was wrong? she wondered. She should feel relieved. She shouldn't be feeling alarmed and panicky, as if something she desperately wanted was about to slip through her fingers. "Yes, I'll be leaving."

"Fine." He moved, heading for his bedroom, talking over his shoulder. "I'll have John bring your car around."

"No, wait!"

He stopped and turned back, his jaw clenched, his muscles tensed. "What?"

She held out the money to him. "I can't take the money for the days I won't be here."

Something flickered in his eyes. "Yes, Emily, you can, because I insist. It's the way I want it." He turned on his heel, strode down the hall to his room, and went in. The door shut quietly behind him.

And Emily was left staring at the money, feeling colder than she ever had in her life.

SEVEN

Emily went back to the florist shop and threw herself into her work with a vengeance. She showed up early every morning, telling both Harriet and herself that she was there to get a first look at the flowers as they arrived from the flower market. She would spend hours creating an arrangement that would draw gasps of admiration from her fellow employees and customers, only to tear it apart in a frenzy and do it again. She was aware Harriet was watching her with concern, but there was nothing she could do or say to reassure the other woman. In rare idle moments she admitted she was also concerned about herself.

No matter how many hours she spent working with the flowers, she found no solace. In fact her nerves seemed to grow worse.

At night she spent her time alternately tossing and turning in bed and pacing the floor of her little apartment. Faint circles formed beneath her eyes. She had to force herself to eat.

A few days after her return to work, she almost jumped out of her skin when her employer thrust a newspaper beneath her nose, happily exclaiming over a picture of Jay and her dancing at the charity function.

Jay looked so handsome and compelling, holding her and gazing down at her with a hot intensity that came across even in black and white. And there she was, wearing the dress he had bought for her, so completely mesmerized by him, she hadn't even seen the flare of the flashbulb.

That day, in an effort to escape the inevitable questions from her coworkers, she left work early and drove to the nursing home. Much to Emily's satisfaction her mother was slowly growing stronger under the devoted attention of Elizabeth and the care of the staff. While Emily was there, she kept the conversation light and a smile on her face. But once she left, the smile faded. She might be able to fool her mother, but she couldn't fool herself. She was miserable.

Thoughts of Jay filled her mind night and day, and she remembered every moment she had spent with him. At times she was certain she was in the midst of a fever; at other times she was certain she was losing her mind.

One stormy night around ten o'clock, just over a week after she had left Jay, she found herself sitting in her car in front of his house, staring at it, aching unbearably. Even though she had spent only a little less than a week in the house, it appeared sweetly familiar to her. But she was under no illusions. It wasn't the house that had brought her here tonight.

It was Jay, and she didn't even know if he was inside.

Though the house sat far back from the street and was surrounded by trees, she could still make out lights through the rain. But lights didn't necessarily mean that Jay was home, she reminded herself.

She groaned. She had to be out of her mind to be here.

She turned off the engine. The rain drummed against the car's roof with a fearsome intensity, but the sound still wasn't as loud as the pounding of her heart. Lord help her, she *had* lost her mind. Why couldn't she forget him? Why did she remember every touch, every kiss? Why did her body burn for more?

She was out of the car before she could stop herself and running up the long drive, and she didn't stop running until she had her finger jammed against the bell.

An agony of longing gripped Emily. Thunder cracked and boomed around her. A dozen lifetimes seemed to pass before John finally opened the door.

His eyes widened in surprise, but he kept his voice even. "Miss Stanton, how nice to see you again."

Her heart was pounding even louder now and she felt as out of breath as if she'd run ten miles. "T-Thank you, John. Is Jay here?"

He nodded. "If you'd like to come in, I'll announce you."

His voice sounded far away to her. She felt almost as if she were in a trance, being pulled forward by an unknown force. She moved into the house, and through a dim haze saw Roberta at the bottom of the stairs, one foot on the first step, a tray in her hands.

When she recognized Emily, she set the tray down on the stairs and hurried toward her. "Why, you're soaking wet, honey. Let me get you a towel."

"It's *Miss Stanton*," John said in a reproving voice to his wife.

Roberta ignored him and took Emily's arm.

"I'm wet?" Emily looked down at herself and saw that her dress was plastered to her. How odd, she thought. She hadn't even felt the rain. She freed herself from Roberta's grasp and wiped a hand over her face, discovering moisture.

"I'll get you a towel," Roberta said again, her expression concerned as she started off.

"No, I'm fine, really. . . . I just want to see Jay. Where is he?"

"If you would like to wait in the drawing room," John said in an excruciatingly dignified tone and gestured toward a door that opened off the hall, "I'll announce you."

"He's up in his bedroom," Roberta said to Emily. "I was just on my way there with coffee for him. Would you like to go on up?"

"I really think it would be best if she would wait in—"

"Stick a dishtowel in it, John," Roberta snapped, then smiled reassuringly at Emily. "You just go on up, honey. And if you two decide later on you want something to eat or drink, let me know."

"Thank you," Emily murmured, moving past the stunned John and up the stairs. She completely sympathized with John because she felt equally stunned. She had no idea what she was going to do once she saw Jay or even what she was going to say. She only knew that some inner compulsion was driving her to him.

Outside his bedroom door she paused. Her heart hammered painfully against her rib cage. Her hand shook as she closed it around the doorknob. She should knock, she thought vaguely, but the agony she would endure during the moments it took him to answer might kill her. Quietly she opened the door and went in.

He was standing by the fireplace, speaking to someone on the phone. The tail of the white shirt he wore had been pulled free of his black slacks, and the top half of the shirt's buttons had been opened. She could see a pair of leather shoes lying on their sides some distance away, as if he had stripped them off and tossed them. A tie he had no doubt been wearing during the day was lying over the back of a chair. His body was angled sideways to her, and she could see a worried expression on his face. She stared hungrily at him, taking in the disorder of his hair and the faint shadow of beard on his jaw. She had tried to fight the need to come here, but now that she was here, she wondered how she would ever be able to go away again.

"Follow up on those numbers I gave you. Caleb can be hard to find, but not impossible. Keep it quiet, though. I don't want to alert too many—"

"Jay." she said softly.

He swung around and saw her. "I've got to go," he muttered, then slammed down the receiver.

Almost immediately, it seemed, he was in front of her, grasping her arms, his expression even more worried than it had been.

"Are you all right?" he asked harshly. "Have you been in an accident?"

Did she really look that bad? she wondered dazedly. "I haven't been in an accident," she said, then tried to come up with an explanation. "It's raining."

"I know." His voice was gruff, and deep lines creased his forehead. He released her arm and took a step away, but his gaze never left her. "Why are you here, Emily?"

It was the same question she had been asking herself, and she didn't have an answer. Not yet. To give herself time, she gestured toward the phone. "I'm sorry if I interrupted something important."

"Forget the phone call," he said impatiently, "and tell me what's wrong."

She released a long, shaky breath. This wasn't going well, but if she'd given the matter any thought at all she could have predicted that it wouldn't. She had walked out on him days ago, and in the intervening time had made no effort to contact him until now, when she had showed up in his bedroom late at night, dripping wet. He had every right to be staring at her as if she belonged in a mental institution. "Nothing. Nothing's wrong." Everything was wrong. In fact, strangely enough, she was having a hard time not crying. She folded her hands together. "How have you been?"

"Lousy, thanks." Abruptly he grabbed her hand and pulled her across the room to the fire, then he disappeared into another room and reappeared with a big, thick towel and thrust it at her. "Dry yourself off. In fact take off your dress, and I'll get you a bathrobe." He started off again.

"Jay."

She had spoken quietly, but he heard and stopped. Dammit to hell, it was the same soft voice he had been hearing every night in his dreams. And that was when he had managed to sleep. The rest of the time he had had to fight visions of her face and body, sweeter and more tempting than life itself.

"What?" he asked roughly. With an exclamation he dragged his hand through his hair. "Damn it, Emily, what *is* it? I've gone half out of my mind this past week without you, and now you show up and you won't tell me why you're here."

That was because she didn't know herself. "Our deal is over, isn't it?"

His mouth tightened with a grim expression. "*Yes*. Is that why you came? You wanted to hear me say one more time that you don't owe me anything else?"

"No." Lord, her chest hurt. The ends of her hair hurt. Her heart hurt. "No."

"Dammit, Emily," he burst out violently, "I'm *dying* here! I look at you and all I want to do is grab you and kiss you until neither one of us remembers why you left in the first place." He balled his hands into fists at his side. "In fact I can guarantee you that's exactly what I'm going to do if you keep standing there. *Tell me what you want!*"

As if the force of his words had sent a strong wind blowing through the room, she swayed. And suddenly she had an answer. "You."

"*What?*" He couldn't trust what he had heard.

"I want you, Jay—more than I want to breathe."

Before her heart could beat again, she was in his arms and his mouth was crushing hers. With a cry of joy she wrapped her arms around his neck and held onto him as tightly as she could. Her relief was enormous, as if a long period of torture had just ended for her. For the moment, at any rate, she was exactly where she wanted to be. In Jay's arms, her heart against his.

Time stopped, and everything became sensation. The heat of Jay's fingers at the buttons of her dress. The warmth of the fire against her leg and side. The electricity as his tongue slid deep in her mouth. She was happy. This was what she had been wanting. *Jay*. She had been wanting Jay.

He was the medicine that would cure her fever. He was the sanity that would clear her mind. He was the man who would enable her to draw her next breath. *Jay*.

He skimmed the soggy dress up her torso and over her head and tossed it somewhere behind her. For an instant she felt cool air against her skin, but then Jay put his hands on her, and she was instantly warmed.

"If you hadn't come here tonight, I would have gone to you tomorrow," he muttered.

"Really?"

"I'd take an oath in blood on it." He dropped with her to the floor until they were kneeling in front of the burning fire. The fire's heat matched the burning she felt inside her and dried the rain from her skin. In fact she wouldn't have been surprised to see steam rising from her. At this moment she felt as if she was the hottest spot in the universe and there was only one thing that could cool her. *Jay*.

He pushed the wet strands of her hair away from her face, his expression fierce and intent. "You have no idea how many times I've driven by your house and the florist shop." His voice was rough with emotion. "The only thing that kept me away was that I was afraid you wouldn't want to see me."

"I might not have. I didn't know what I wanted until tonight." She started on the buttons of his shirt that remained fastened. In the days she had spent here with him, she had often been tempted to run her hands across his chest, but she had always stopped herself. Tonight she was determined to do anything she wished. And she wished very much to explore his body.

When he felt the light touch of her hand smoothing across his chest, he gave a loud groan. "Lord, it's been hell without you."

"I know," she said softly. "I was in the same hell."

Vaguely he supposed that he should question the reasoning behind her change of mind, to try to make sense out of what was happening. But he found he didn't give a damn. She was here with him, her fingers touching him, her eyes full of desire for him. She wanted him, and God knew he wanted her, beyond the point of distraction, beyond the point of reason. His loins were already engorged and throbbing. His mind had already shut down.

He quickly shrugged out of his shirt, then laid her back on the thick white carpet. No doubt he should carry her over to the bed, but he couldn't force himself to take the time. The carpet was soft, and the fire had made it warm, and a driving urgency was pounding through his blood. He had her beneath him now, and he couldn't let her go.

He leaned over and whispered, "Arch your back for me."

She did, and he reached beneath her and unhooked her bra, freeing her breasts. The bra vanished, and without waiting for what he would do next, she reached for him, framing his face with her hands, then pulling his head down until he fastened his mouth around one tightly beaded nipple. At the contact she let out a moan of pleasure.

His mouth sucked and pulled at the taut peak, while his hand molded and caressed. Again and again her stomach contracted. She had thought she had learned desire from his kisses, but on the floor in front of the fire he taught her new definitions, new parameters.

Touch by touch, he tore through restraints. Kiss by kiss, he overcame barriers. Somehow, at some time, her panties and his clothes disappeared. His nakedness made her forget her own. His skin was smooth, bronzed, and glistening in the light from the fire; his stomach was muscled and flat; and lower, his sex was blatantly full and thick. New desire exploded in her, but it wasn't to be sated yet.

He was a detail man, she had known it from the beginning. But she hadn't considered how the trait would affect their lovemaking, how the attention he paid to each part of her body would soften her bones and heat her blood to boiling, how his lips and hands could create feelings of such immense proportion, she was sure she wouldn't be able to contain them all.

And when at last he parted her legs, she was already clawing at his back, her fingers digging into the muscles that rippled there.

"Easy," he whispered. "Easy. I'm afraid this is going to hurt."

She was already hurting, and she was ready to do anything to get relief. But it was a shock to feel him between her legs, and an even greater shock when he began to push into her. She went still. He felt so big, for a moment she wasn't sure she could accommodate him. Kissing her, he murmured encouraging, reassuring words, and gradually she began to relax again.

Little by little he eased into her. It was hard for him to go slow. As each moment passed, the danger grew greater that his control would slip, but he was determined that even though there might be pain for her this first time, there would also be pleasure. He could feel her stretching to take him in and knew the instant the pain began. With a muttered curse to himself, then a soft endearment to her, he drew back his hips and deliberately pushed into her, forcing himself through the thin obstruction of her maidenhead until he was deep inside her as far as he could go. "Are you all right?" he asked harshly.

"Yes," she said on a half sob. There had been pain, but already she could feel the stirrings of pleasure. And the pleasure far outweighed the pain. Instinctively she began to move, arching against him, taking him deeper into her. To do so was a compulsion she couldn't fight. She had no control over her actions. Her longing for him knew no bounds. It seemed the rhythm of their two entwined bodies moving together had been predestined.

Sensation piled on sensation until she was frantic.

She held back nothing. If he cared to take a look, she thought, it was entirely possible that he would be able to see everything that was inside her, every need, every wish. But he wouldn't see fear, not at this moment. A fiery desire had seared it out of her.

She writhed and twisted beneath him, feeling as if she were burning from the inside out. She slid her hands down his back and pressed them against his buttocks, urging him to move faster. She was being filled up with heat and Jay until she thought she couldn't take anymore. He had always been incredibly gentle with her, and she could tell he was trying not to hurt her now. But there was something fierce and primal in him that matched what was in her, and they had both reached the point where neither one of them was capable of being denied.

Her release came suddenly, taking her by surprise, catching her in a whirlpool that had her spinning wildly toward a dark, ecstatic unknown. She clung to Jay and called out his name in an unguarded, soul-exposing way she had never said another person's name.

His name and the feel of her tiny, inner muscles contracting around him sent him out of control. He drove into her hard, using all his strength, and he exploded in a climax more powerful and mind-shattering than anything he had ever known.

He rolled to his side, but he didn't break away from her immediately. He stayed inside her and held her to him, waiting for his breathing to return to normal. It seemed to take a long time. Saturated with contentment, he held her to him while the fire's warmth dried the sweat on their entwined bodies. After a while he reluctantly loosened himself from her, surged to his feet, threw several more logs on the fire, then reached for her and drew her upright and into his arms. He carried her to the bed and settled on it with her. Without any prompting from him, she snuggled beside him, her head on his shoulders.

He waited until he thought he could speak without his voice wavering, then he murmured, "I can't tell you how glad I am that you decided to come back tonight."

Her mouth curved only slightly upward, but it was more because she lacked the energy than the will to smile. In truth she could never remember feeling such peacefulness. "I'm glad too."

"First thing in the morning we'll go get your things."

The steely possessiveness in his voice didn't escape her, but it also didn't bother her. At the moment she didn't feel she had a nerve in her body. "I'm not staying."

He stiffened. "What?"

Her eyes drifted closed. "I'll stay the night, but I have to go to work in the morning."

"But you'll come back tomorrow night, won't you?"

She yawned and snuggled more closely against him. "I really haven't thought that far ahead."

He abruptly shifted away from her. Startled, she opened her eyes to see him above her, his eyes glittering fiercely. "You're not leaving me again."

She sighed. "You have to understand," she said quietly. "I can't become your mistress."

His frown was darkly ominous. "Who the hell said anything about you being my mistress? Haven't you ever heard of two people living together because they don't want to live apart?"

She looked at him for a long moment, then lifted her hand and lightly traced her fingers along the lines of his frown. "I didn't make the decision to come here tonight, Jay. The decision made itself, and suddenly I was here. What happened between us tonight was momentous. You were the first. You'll probably be the only and the last. But I need time to deal with it. Chances are I may never see you again after tonight. I—"

"You're wrong," he said, sharply cutting through her words. "I agree what happened tonight was momentous, but you will see me again. It can be on your terms—make them up, I'll agree to anything." He saw her tense. "And I'm *not* talking about money. If it were up to me, you'd never want for anything, but because it's important to you, that aspect has to be up to you." He took her hand and brought it to his mouth for a kiss. "But, Emily, don't even try to disappear from my life again. I wouldn't be able to stand it."

Oddly enough she understood. She didn't think she

would be able to stand being apart from him, either, but she also knew she couldn't go back to the way things had been between them before. She couldn't allow herself to be at his beck and call. She had to maintain her independence. Otherwise his energy and power just might swallow her up and she would disappear forever.

"I'll stay tonight," she said. "In the morning I'll go to work. After that we'll see."

"Yes," he muttered huskily, "we'll see."

He woke her several times in the night, and their lovemaking was just as fierce and as wild as it had been the first time, their need for each other just as great. By morning Emily was sore and pleasantly exhausted, but she was also thoroughly satisfied in every cell of her body. So much so that her continued desire for him mystified her. She didn't understand why she could still want him, still thrill at his touch, still hunger for his kisses, still desperately need him inside her again and again. She just knew she did

They showered together and made love once more. Then somehow she gathered the strength to go to work. But as each hour passed, she grew more and more eager to see him again. She was obviously in the midst of a delirium, she decided, and for the moment she didn't see any way out of it. She also couldn't see any reason why she should fight it. Her mother was safe and well cared for, and for the foreseeable future her money worries were under control.

For the time being, she decided, she could afford to let herself wallow in this delirium of passion she felt for Jay. It wouldn't last of course. Something would happen to dissipate the power of the passion and cool their fever for each other.

He would grow tired of her, or she would decide it was time to call a halt to it. But as long as she kept her heart intact, she saw no reason why she couldn't enjoy herself, at least for a while longer.

EIGHT

Emily spent the next few nights with Jay at his house. Each night they would make love, and each morning she and Jay would come down to find the breakfast table set for two. Roberta generally stayed in the kitchen, though she would occasionally pop out to inquire what they would like to eat for the next meal. Poor Roberta, Emily reflected wryly Friday morning as she sat across the breakfast table from Jay. Roberta spent hours preparing their meals, but as wonderful as the dishes she turned out were, food was not uppermost in either of their minds.

She cast a surreptitious glance his way. The thickness of his dark lashes was displayed as he scanned the morning paper with lowered eyes. She wasn't actually living with him, as she had the first time. Each evening she would go home and get a fresh set of clothes. Still, she was fully aware that she was maintaining only a veneer of independence. But however slight the distinction between living with him and merely spending a succession of nights with him, it was terribly important to her.

Intimacy was so new to her. And alien. After spending hours in the night learning the secrets of each other's bodies, she supposed it was only natural that she be more comfortable with him in the daylight. But she never for a moment took what was happening between them for granted. She knew how fast life could throw you curves and how things could change for the worse with lightning speed. Even so, something as simple and as casual as sitting across the breakfast table from him was to be wondered at.

"How are you doing for time?" Jay asked.

She glanced at her watch. "I'd better run soon. We're doing flowers for two weddings today. It's going to be busy."

"What about tomorrow?"

"Saturday?" She shrugged. "I don't think we have any special orders. Why?"

"Because I was wondering if you could get the day off. Maybe Monday too. I'd like us to go on a little holiday."

"A holiday?" She repeated the word and still couldn't decide what he meant.

"Remember when I asked if you'd ever been on a vacation and you said no? Well, I'd like to take you on one. Just for a few days."

"Where?"

"I have a cabin in Colorado. You'll love it. It's miles from anyone, and at night there are more stars than you've ever seen in your life."

"Stars," she said softly. "It sounds wonderful."

"Then let's go. We can fly out tonight after work."

Instantly her guard came up—for a number of reasons. "I've never flown before. I've never even *thought* about flying."

"I can promise you'll arrive safe and sound."

Her lips twisted wryly. "You may own your own plane, Jay, but I doubt if even you can control weather conditions or prevent mechanical failures."

"I can't control weather conditions, but I can and do hire the best pilot available to chart a course around bad weather, plus I employ the best mechanics in the business to make sure there are *no* mechanical problems with the jet. Come on, Emily. Besides work, you don't have any reason to stay in town this weekend, do you?"

She had one very good reason: her mother. She might be receiving excellent care, but she was still hesitant to leave town. She liked to know that she was close in case anything happened. But then she supposed she could check in by phone. . . ."I don't know."

"What's keeping you from saying yes?"

She couldn't help but smile. "Things are so simple for you, aren't they? When you're presented with an obstacle, your first instinct is to tear right through it."

"Yes, it is. But to do that, I first have to understand what the obstacle is. With you, I've never known."

Her smile faded. "Let me think about it and talk to Harriet. Maybe I can get off, but we'd probably have to be back by Monday."

He smiled. "I'll meet you at your place after work."

Emily walked out onto the patio of the nursing home and spied her mother sitting in the sun in a wheelchair, a pink ribbon tied in a bow around her gray hair. The sight made her heart warm with gladness. "Well, look at you," she exclaimed, walking over to her. "You're sitting up and you look so pretty." She was wearing one of the new robes Emily had bought her, a pink cotton one with tiny flowers embroidered on it.

Her mother's face lit up when she saw her. "I didn't expect to see you today."

Emily drew up a chair and sat down. "I decided to come over on my lunch hour. There's a possibility I may go out of town for a couple of days, and I wanted to check on you." Actually Harriet had already said she could have the time off. Now she had to decide if she felt all right about leaving her mother, plus whether she wanted to spend a whole weekend of uninterrupted, close, intimate contact with Jay. It would be a risk, but since she had met Jay, there hadn't been a day that hadn't been filled with risks.

"That's wonderful, darling. Are you going with the same girlfriend you went with before?"

"Yes, yes, I am." Her mother would only worry about her if she knew the truth. "But if I go, I'll be back Monday."

"Go. Have fun. You're looking so much better, more rested."

Emily chuckled. "Let me return the compliment. You actually have color in your cheeks. This place is good for you, isn't it?"

Her mother nodded. "I'm so happy that I'm getting stronger. I want to get a job as soon as I can so that I can relieve you of the burden you've been under with my hospital expenses."

The doctors she had spoken with hadn't been able to tell her if her mother would ever recover to the point where she could work, but she chose not to tell her that. "Don't worry about it. I'm managing fine. Listen, Mom, there's something I need to ask you. My picture was in the paper a few days ago—"

"It was?" her mother asked excitedly. "Why? Where is it? I want to see it."

"I don't have a copy with me, but I'll try to remember to bring one next time." In the meantime she'd come up with a story about who Jay was that would satisfy her mother. "It was no big deal, just a party I attended, but I've been worried that Ralph would see it and find out that we're here. Has there been any sign of him?"

The light died out of her mother's eyes, and she shook her head. "None, and I don't really see anything to worry about. After all, he's down in Houston."

"Good. I hope he stays there. But I don't underestimate him. He's crafty and mean as a snake. If you'd only get a divorce—"

"I can't, Emily. We were married in the church."

"That doesn't give him the right to beat you, Mom." Actually she wasn't sure even a legal divorce would free her mother of the man. That's why she was trying so hard to keep their whereabouts a secret. "Anyway," she said with a sigh, "just in case, I've asked Mrs. Thompson to notify me if you have any visitors."

The older woman's hands moved in an agitated manner. "Emily, it's been months. I think we're safe."

She reached over and took one of her hands. "I hope you're right, I really do."

That afternoon Emily arrived home to find Jay waiting for her on the porch with a garment bag and a suitcase.

"I hope you were able to get off," he said, greeting her with a kiss.

"I was," she said, casting a suspicious look at the leather bags. "Whose are those?"

"Relax. I would have bought you your own set of luggage if I had thought you would accept it, but I knew you wouldn't. These bags are mine. I brought them for you to use this weekend."

Emily understood that it went against the grain with Jay to make allowances for her need to feel independent. He had made it plain that he would rather she quit work, move in with him, and let him buy her rooms full of clothes, jewelry, and suitcases. Because she appreciated his effort, she graced him with a smile. "You have something against paper bags?"

His eyes twinkled. "Just call me ecologically minded. I think the fewer paper products we use, the better off we'll be."

"I recycle."

He sighed. "Use the bags, Emily."

With a laugh she went to pack, and soon they were flying high above the clouds in the sleek jet owned by Jay. She was nervous during takeoff, but Jay held her hand and talked her through it, and gradually she forgot all about being anxious.

They had dinner on the plane and a couple of hours later landed on a private airstrip in the mountains just as the sun was setting. The air was crisp and sparkling clean, and the fantastic view seemed to stretch to forever.

They climbed into a four-wheel-drive vehicle that had been parked in a shelter at the strip and drove several miles up a private road. The jet took off behind them, circled, then headed off.

Jay pulled to a stop in front of a two-story house that looked as if it had been grown by nature rather than been built by man. Its sprawling rustic splendor blended seamlessly into its equally dramatic surroundings.

Emily managed to keep quiet until she was standing in the center of the two-story-high main room. "Is this really the place you were referring to when you said you had a cabin?"

He chuckled. "Well, it is made out of logs."

"Right." Cedar logs, polished oak flooring, and gleaming birch-and-cedar paneling. More than that, from its flannel-covered sofas and chairs to the stone fireplace and valuable artwork on the walls, its homey feeling was the result of every bit as much attention to detail as the house in Dallas. "You decorated this, didn't you?"

He shrugged. "I don't *decorate*. I just buy things I like and put them where I think they look nice. Do you like it?"

"It's fabulous, but it's hard for me to grasp that someone doesn't live here year-round, that you come here only occasionally. It seems like such a waste."

"Not really. I get here quite a bit, even if it's only for a weekend like this time. But I understand what you mean."

"You do?"

"Sure. Until about fifteen years ago I had never had a real home. Trust me, I'm not so jaded that I don't understand how lucky I am to have not just one, but several beautiful homes."

Her eyes widened. "You have more than the two I've seen?"

"I have one on the island of Mustique. I'll take you there soon."

Just for a moment she allowed herself to envision them together on a tropical island playing in the surf or walking in the moonlight. But then she got hold of her emotions. She had to be realistic, she reminded herself. She couldn't take him seriously when he said things like that. Whether it was because of her wishes or because of his, they would be parting before too very long. She bit down on her bottom lip until the physical pain drove away the pain that seemed centered near her heart.

"Do you have a staff here?" She had barely seen the pilot who had flown them here, and she hadn't seen anyone else since they had landed.

"Not a permanent one. I keep the Jeep at the airstrip, so that no one has to meet me and I can get around on my own. A lady who lives in the nearest town drives out here and cleans every couple of weeks. And when I know I'm coming, I call ahead, and she stocks the kitchen with staples. Also every time I come, Roberta sends me with several coolers' worth of food for the freezer. I don't starve."

"It doesn't look as if you rough it either."

"Not any more. I consider my first twenty years rough enough for a lifetime."

"What do you mean?"

He looked at her. "Are you interested?"

She rolled her shoulders. "Slightly curious, that's all."

"Then I'll tell you about it sometime." He took her hand. "Come on. I'll show you upstairs."

The upstairs contained the large master bedroom. One entire wall was windows that looked out over a far-reaching vista of mountains, trees, and sky. The bed faced the windows.

"It's incredibly beautiful," she said, her voice hushed and reverent as she walked to the window. "It makes me feel good that a place like this actually exists on earth, and yet it makes me want to cry."

"Why?" He put their bags down and came up behind her.

"I don't know. Silly, isn't it?"

"No." He put his hands on her shoulders and drew her back so that her body rested against his. "Don't get defensive, because this is just a guess, but up to now you probably haven't had the opportunity to see any mountains."

"I haven't. When you live in a gutter, it's hard to believe that there are mountains like these and that they could possibly be so beautiful."

He bent his head and pressed his face against hers. "Want to tell me about that gutter?" he asked softly.

"No." Her voice was sharper than before. "It was only a metaphor anyway.

"I know." He lifted his head away and smoothed his hand over her silky hair. "I didn't really believe you lived in an actual gutter. It just felt to you like you did."

He sounded as if he understood, she thought, but she was really going to have to do a better job of guarding herself. Sometimes he came precariously close to the center of her soul.

"But even if you couldn't see mountains, you believed they were here."

"How do you know?"

"Because you believe a tree makes a noise when it falls."

"I said I *want* to believe it does. That's different. It's a *need* to believe, more than an absolute concrete belief."

"You can appreciate the mountains to a certain extent in pictures, but until you see it in person, you can't imagine the grandeur. And when you do see it for the first time, it takes your breath away. It certainly does mine. Every time I come here, it's like I'm seeing them all over again for the first time." He turned her to him. "It's like kissing you. Every time I do, it's like I'm kissing you for the first time. I never get over the wonder." He dropped a light kiss on her lips. "And I never seem to get enough of you."

Heat welled up in her, as did emotions too complicated to sort out for the moment. "Would you like to watch the sun set from the bed?"

"I can't think of anything I'd rather do."

* * *

She completely missed the setting of the sun. She was too absorbed in the things Jay was doing to her body to notice. They spent the evening in bed, leaving it only long enough to heat up one of Roberta's casseroles and eat it. Then they came back to bed and made love until they fell asleep, their arms and legs entangled, their bodies pressed intimately together.

The morning sun found them exploring the land around Jay's house. In the afternoon they stopped and rested on a large rock slab that was positioned to give them a glorious view. A golden eagle soared on the wind currents above the valley below them.

"I can't get over this place."

"I knew you'd love it if I ever got you here." He had propped one hand on his drawn-up knee. He was wearing a lightweight green-flannel plaid shirt open over a white T-shirt, and blue jeans clad his muscled thighs and calves. He looked incredibly virile and sexy.

"I didn't even put up a fight."

"You thought about it, though."

She laughed. "Yeah, I did."

"I'm glad you didn't. I wanted to bring you here, but I also badly needed to come myself."

"Why's that?"

"Every so often I have to get away from the crap and game playing that goes on in business. This place refreshes me."

She remembered the look of worry she had seen on his face when she had walked into his bedroom that stormy night about a week ago. She had forgotten about it almost immediately. The following hours had seared away all thoughts from her mind. When he was with her, he had a way of concentrating so totally on her that she forgot any and all other things. But now . . . "Are you having a problem?"

He grinned as if he enjoyed the thought of the problem. "You could say that. When I came along, I busted up the monopoly the big boys have held on the telecommunications field for so many years. Now after months of negotiation I'm about to get a huge new contract that will give me an even greater slice of the pie, and they're feeling threatened."

She looked at him closely. He didn't seem particularly worried. "What do you mean?"

"For some time now there have been rumors floating around that my company was about to be served with an injunction, and yesterday it happened. They're saying that one of my key patents infringes on another patent, an obscure one. I've got one week to disprove their claim, or they're going to shut me down."

She stared at him, stunned. "What could happen if they do that?"

"The worst-case scenario is that my customers will lose confidence and start pulling the plug on us. I'll lose my lines of credit, and my stock will plummet. At the best it's a huge delaying tactic that could cost me millions."

She sat up straighter. "Then what in the world are you doing here with me? Why aren't you back in Dallas trying to disprove their claim?"

"Because I really wanted to come here with you, and because I've got people working on the problem." His gaze followed the eagle as it glided on the wind. "They're trying to find someone for me, a man named Caleb McClintock. The problem is, he's not always easy to find. But if I can find him, I may have my problem solved." He flashed another grin. "I think the big boys have once again underestimated me."

How could anyone possibly underestimate him? she wondered. Set against the power and might of the mountains, his inherent power was intensified, not diminished. And she wasn't amazed. To her mind he was as primal a force as the rugged peaks around them.

She had fought against her curiosity for as long as she could, but she finally succumbed. "You said you had a rough life, but that didn't stop you from climbing to the top in your field. How did you do it?"

He switched his gaze to her and regarded her thoughtfully. "How much do you want to know? In other words, how far do you want me to go back?"

Knowledge of him would take her to a new level of intimacy, but she wanted to know. "As far back as you think you need to go for me to understand."

"Then I'd have to start with my mother's death from cancer when I was two. That left my father and me, but I guess he didn't feel emotionally up to raising a child on his own. Or maybe he was just a bum—I don't know. Anyway, for reasons I'm sure only he really understood, he gave me up."

How sad, she thought, but then it could have been worse for him. He could have been raised in an abusive home, as she had been.

"I was raised in a series of foster homes."

"Were they kind to you, these people?"

He shrugged. "They weren't necessarily unkind, but things happen when there's no one to love a child. They also *don't* happen, and sometimes it's not anybody's fault. I hated not having a home or a family. I never felt I belonged. I was always left feeling as if I was on the outside looking in. And I was always cold—emotionally, physically, you name it. I guess that's one of the reasons I love fires so much."

Like her, she realized, he had never experienced a happy home or family. Like her he had felt isolated and lonely. Like her he was scarred on the inside. And so as soon as he was able, he had created his own homes, like his house here and the one in Dallas. Both looked as if they belonged to a family. No doubt he was simply waiting for the right woman to come along to start his family, a woman without scars to bear his children and be his wife.

He went on. "I figured out early that education would be my way out. It was a long, hard struggle at times, but I aced all my classes and, with scholarships and grants, put myself through college. When I graduated, I went to work for a blue-chip company that had recruited me. But before I did, I made I deal with them. I would work for them for a certain number of years, designing for them, but then they would provide venture capital to help me start up my own company. They were happy because they made money with me, and I was happy because I was finally able to live life on my own terms."

He was extraordinary. There wasn't a moment she had known him that she hadn't thought it. His accomplishments were amazing, all the more so because of the shark-infested waters of business he had had to swim in. She remembered her first impression of him, that he had clawed and scratched his way through life, and despite tremendous odds had endured. She had been right. "Did you ever make an effort after you were grown to find your father?"

"Yeah. I found him in a cemetery in Oregon. He had died about five years after he gave me up. I don't know of what. I decided it didn't matter."

Somehow she knew that it had mattered to him. He must have felt abandoned. She had. After her father had died, her mother had fallen apart, and for a while it had been as if she had lost two parents. She had not only felt abandoned, she had felt confused and scared. Then Ralph had entered her life, and she had come to hate him. She knew firsthand how mixed up children's emotions could be about their parents. "And now you're here. And from up here it looks like the whole world is spread out below your feet. It must be a tremendous feeling."

"It's a humbling feeling. Very humbling."

His reaction surprised her. "I would think it would make some men feel extremely powerful."

He chuckled. "You're probably right. In fact I do business with a few of those very men."

She brushed a wind-tossed strand of hair away from her face. "But I would think if anyone felt that way, you should. Everything you've done has been because of your own drive and talent. You deserve to feel tremendous satisfaction."

"Nothing is completely simple, but yeah, I do feel satisfaction, among other things."

"What other things?"

"Determination to hang on to what I have and then to go on and accomplish more."

She reached out and touched his face. "You'll do it. Whatever you want to do, you'll do it."

He would remember this moment forever, he thought. Emily touching him, with the wind in her hair and the sun gilding her skin. She looked sexy and beautiful and in that moment he knew he was hopelessly in love with her. Hopelessly. "Do you really believe that?" he asked huskily.

"Yes, I do."

"Then you must feel in grave danger, because one of the things I want is you."

Where once she might have run at such a statement, now she smiled. "Let me tell you something—I've felt in grave danger ever since I first saw you. And by the way, you already have me."

"Part of you, but I want the rest of you too."

She gave a laugh. "You have the best part, the part that is free of complications. Be grateful."

"I want all of you."

She lay back on the slab of warm stone and stretched. "No one gets everything they want."

"*I* will."

She turned her head so that she could see him outlined against the deep-blue sky. "Shut up, Jay, and make love to me."

"Here?"

"Why not?"

"This rock is hard."

She smiled. "That's why you're going to be on the bottom."

"Emily," he said, expelling a harsh breath as he went down to her, "you excite the hell out of me."

NINE

She was as close as she had ever come to feeling contentment about her life, Emily thought later that night as she lay beside Jay on a wide lounger out on one of the house's many decks. Oh, it wouldn't last. But while this feeling of utter satisfaction and peace was with her, she was going to savor it, because, quite simply, she had no idea when it would come again.

"I've never seen so many stars."

Jay waved his hand toward the sky. "I ordered them up just for you."

"It looks as if I could dip a ladle into the sky and come back with it full."

"Go ahead."

She chuckled. "I said it *looked* as if I could."

"You're not going to even try?"

Her expression turned incredulous. "Where is that naïveté coming from? I know you didn't get where you are today by being someone who believes you can scoop stars out of the sky."

"I got where I am today by disregarding limits and boundaries of any kind. If I'd ever wanted a ladleful of stars, I would have at least tried."

"And you probably would have succeeded," she said, amused. "I guess I stand corrected."

"Tell me what you want, Emily."

Her brow knitted with puzzlement. "Haven't we already been through this?"

"To a point. You wanted the money and you wanted me—"

"As I recall, more than I wanted to breathe."

Her soft voice had heat pooling in his loins. "*Don't* distract me."

"Could I?" she asked with a touch of mischievousness.

He took her hand, brought it to his lips, and pressed a kiss to its back. "I'm here with you during one of the biggest crises of my career, aren't I?"

"Yes," she said, suddenly serious, "and I don't think you should be."

"Never mind that. The point is, you *can* distract me. *Easily.* Let's get back to what else it is you want."

She had no idea why he was asking, but she nevertheless dutifully pondered his question. Before she had met him, she had never thought even a minute's worth of the contentment she was feeling was possible for her. And before she had met him, she hadn't seen how she was going to be able to provide the medical care her mother so badly needed. After those two things, she decided, there wasn't anything else she needed. She spread her hands apart. "I can't think of a thing."

"Nothing?"

"No."

"Then you're an unusual person."

"No, just practical. The money you gave me . . . has helped me enormously." Her hesitation had been due to the fact that, even though she had done nothing more than state the obvious, it was still more than she had told him before. "I don't believe in being greedy."

"You could have gotten three times that amount," he murmured. "Hell, four or five times. You still could."

Her teeth came together. "I won't take any more money from you, Jay, and I don't even want to talk about it."

"Okay, but aren't you going to ask what *I* want?"

"I know what you want. You want to keep what you already have—which, by the way, you'll have more success at if you stop trying to give it all to me—and you want to find a man named Caleb."

"You forgot one very important thing that I want. In fact it's the most important thing."

"What?" she asked curiously.

"You. I want you."

She was beginning to get annoyed. "Good grief, Jay. We've been through this too. You *have* me."

"No, you don't understand. I'm trying to tell you something, and I'm doing a really bad job of it."

She eyed him warily. "I won't enter into another deal with you, Jay, so you can just forget it."

"Forget deals. Forget money. This is about you and me. I love you, Emily. I love you and I want you to love me."

She wasn't even aware that she had moved until she was suddenly standing at the edge of the deck, her back to the rail, and there was several feet between them.

She had known it would happen. She had known that in a fraction of a moment her contentment would be shattered. She just hadn't known how or why it would happen. "Don't love me, Jay. *Don't.* I *forbid* you to."

He pushed up from the lounge and slowly walked to her. "That's a really interesting order, Emily. How do you propose I carry it out when I'm already so much in love with you I can't see straight?"

Tears sprang to her eyes, and her heart began to pound with fear. "You just *stop,* that's all. Just *stop.* I don't want you to love me. I don't want to be loved!"

He gazed at her for a long moment. "Everyone wants to be loved."

"You're very wrong! *I* don't!"

"Then we have a serious problem, because I can't stop loving you."

"Damn you, Jay! Why couldn't we have continued on as we have been for a little while longer? Why did you have to ruin it?" She waved a wild hand toward the house. "Your homes look as if they're just *waiting* for a family to walk into them, but I'm not going to be that family for you. I can't!"

"Why?"

"Because love is a trap!"

"A trap? You consider love a trap?"

"Yes!" The shrill sound of a phone ringing sliced into her nerves.

"I'm sorry," he said, clearly frustrated at the interruption. "I have to get that. No one would call here unless it was important. I'll be right back."

Emily stayed where she was after he had disappeared into the house, immobilized by an unreasoning fear and an overwhelming anguish. No one knew better than she that happiness wasn't to be trusted. And love *definitely* wasn't. She had seen the things people did in the name of love. Her mother had chained herself emotionally to a man for over twenty years because she loved him and had vowed in a church to remain with him until her death. And Ralph had done his best to oblige her, nearly killing her time and again because he "loved" her so very much.

The whole idea of love frightened Emily to her bones, but her course was clear. When they got back to Dallas, she and Jay would have to go their separate ways. She would not be bound by love to anyone, even if that person was Jay, even if the idea of parting from him was tearing her heart out.

She looked up to see Jay striding back out onto the deck, and remarkably he had a smile on his face.

"My assistant thinks he's found Caleb. The people around Caleb are notorious for stonewalling on his whereabouts, or anything else about him for that matter, but my assistant has finally found someone who has admitted that he thinks he knows where Caleb will be tomorrow evening."

"He *thinks*?"

"With Caleb that's the best we can hope for." He shrugged. "He has a tendency to become absorbed in something and forget when and where he's supposed to be."

"So where is he supposed to be tomorrow night?"

"L.A. Want to go?"

Her mouth dropped open. "Los Angeles? No. I told you I'd need to be back by Monday."

He moved closer to her, and his voice softened to a coaxing tone. "And you will be. I promise. We're just going to make a detour. It's important that I talk to Caleb."

She knew it was important, and she gave a reluctant nod. No matter what, she didn't want Jay to lose his company.

"See," he said softly. "I just got one of the things I had been wanting—Caleb. Now there's only one other thing left that I want. *You*. And if you think I don't plan to get you, then you haven't gotten to know me very well."

There was an intent behind his words that sent a shiver through her. "Look, Jay—"

He pulled her against him and slid his fingers through her hair, combing it back from her face. "Would you like to tell me why you think love is a trap?"

"It just is, that's all."

"You can't explain?"

"I don't want to." What would be the use? she thought. They would only end up arguing, and she didn't want to spend the few precious hours they had left fighting.

"Okay, then, I'll let it go for now. So how would you like to make love beneath the stars?"

The warmth from his body had worked its way into her, but she managed to keep her gaze defiant. "I don't love you, Jay."

Gently smiling, he leaned down and pressed a soft kiss to her lips. "That wasn't the question," he murmured, keeping his mouth close to hers so that when she breathed, he could feel its warmth. "The question was, how would you like to make love beneath the stars?" He unbuttoned her blouse and slipped his hand inside her bra.

"I—"

"Please say yes," he whispered. "I need you. I can't even begin to tell you how much."

She threaded her fingers up through his hair and pulled his head down so that his mouth was crushed against hers, and then she moaned as the familiar ecstasy closed around her. He could make desire flame in her as easily as lighting a match. He could make her worries and fears fade until there was nothing left in her but a clawing need for him. And right now that was all she wanted to feel.

As he caressed and kneaded her breast, his palm scraped back and forth over her nipple, and her breasts swelled, filling his hand. He knew how to give her pleasure in amounts she had never thought possible. She might not love him, but she wanted him. And right now she wanted nothing more than to make love beneath the stars.

She tugged him toward the wide, padded lounger, pushed him back onto it, and went down into his waiting arms.

Jay didn't bring up the subject of love again, and Emily didn't either. If their time together was about to come to an end, then she preferred that their last hours be spent amiably.

Around six the next evening they flew into the Burbank airport, and a waiting limousine whisked them out onto the Los Angeles freeway system and headed for downtown Los Angeles.

"Dodger Stadium?" she asked dubiously when she finally thought to ask exactly where they were going. "This Caleb person who is so important to you is at Dodger Stadium?"

"According to my sources, he's reserved almost an entire section on the top deck."

"He sounds very strange." Her comment was idle and offhand. In truth she was having trouble thinking about anyone but Jay. He was wearing jeans shrinked to fit his muscled thighs to perfection, a blue open-necked sports shirt that revealed the strong column of his throat, and a lightweight navy jacket. Simply looking at him filled her with a curling warmth. She never tired of looking at him, never tired of making love with him. If he had pulled her to him and demanded they make love right there and then, she would have gladly complied. She could only conclude that her eagerness was directly attributable to the fact that she would soon be turning her back on him and walking away from him forever.

"*Unique* is the word," he said, his gaze level on her, a small smile playing around his lips, as if he knew exactly what she was thinking. "He's *totally* unique, very much an eccentric and absolutely brilliant. He holds some of the most important patents ever designed in the field of telecommunications, medicine, and electronics."

"And he likes baseball?"

"He likes baseball, but he *loves* rock and roll and the blues. Always has. And as it happens, Eric Clapton and Elton John are playing a double bill at the stadium tonight."

"Oh." She had never been to a concert before, but

then, she thought, this trip had turned out to be filled with firsts. Her first plane ride, her first limousine ride, her first time to see mountains and an eagle, her first time to see dense thickets of stars in a black-velvet sky.

And then there was the first that eclipsed all other firsts—the first time a man had ever told her he loved her.

And because he had, sadly, it would also be a trip of *lasts*.

The limousine driver pulled the long car into the parking lot and waited in a line of similar-length cars until he could get them as near to the entrance as possible.

Many sets of steps and stairs later, they were at the top of the stadium, and Emily's legs were hurting from the climb. But the view was spectacular. If she looked one way, she could see Los Angeles spread out before her; if she looked the other way she saw the inside of the stadium with its sold-out crowd. Even more remarkable, she saw one man standing on a huge stage in center field, and he was playing the most soulful guitar music she had ever heard.

Jay took her hand and led her down a steep incline of concrete stairs to the man who sat all alone in the middle of an empty section. The elusive Caleb, she presumed.

He was good-looking, she decided, in a rather interesting fashion, with his longish hair pulled back into a ponytail and wire-rimmed glasses perched low on his nose. He was wearing a Grateful Dead T-shirt that boasted several holes, faded blue jeans with even more holes, and once-white-now-dirt-colored tennis shoes, which were propped on the seat in front of him. An expensive-looking black jacket had been flung over the back of a nearby seat in such a way that its label showed. Armani, it said. There was a notepad in his lap on which he had drawn a complicated set of lines and symbols, and he was staring intently down at the stage, a totally engrossed expression on his face.

A redhead with legs as long as California and a tan too perfect for nature to have created sat beside him. Her shapely arms were encircled with enough gold to help balance the national budget, and her drastically short skirt had more than one male in the area interested. But as far as Emily could see, Caleb wasn't even aware the girl was beside him.

Jay dropped down in a seat, leaving one empty chair between him and Caleb, and drew her down into a seat on the other side of him.

Emily waited for Caleb to acknowledge their presence, and when he didn't, she leaned over and spoke into Jay's ear. "Aren't you going to say anything to him, tell him we're here, *something*?"

With a smile he shook his head and put his arm around her shoulders. "He knows we're here, and he'll talk to me when he's ready. Until then just relax and enjoy the concert."

It wasn't a hard thing to do, she decided. Eric Clapton's music alternately thundered and seared out of center field. He played the blues like a man well acquainted with the emotion, and he played rock and roll with a passion that seemed as if it could part the heavens with its strength. She was caught and held by his music, not just because of his instrumental prowess but because the passion and blues of his music moved her. Almost as much as the man sitting beside her moved her.

Weeks ago she might not have been able to connect with the music, but tonight, on the last night she ever planned to spend with Jay, she could and did. The emotion-filled chords Clapton played touched similar chords inside her, and as the time passed, she found her head on Jay's shoulder and her eyes shimmering with tears. A trip of *lasts*.

By the time Clapton finished, the sky had turned to night and the moon had risen over a line of distant palm trees that she could see above the stadium's rim. When Clapton left the stage for the last time and the lights came up, she gave a murmur of surprise.

Jay kissed her temple and released her. "Did you like it?"

"Very much."

He nodded toward the stage. "They'll be setting up for Elton John now. It'll probably take them a half hour or so. While I'm talking to Caleb, think about whether you want to stay for his set or go on home. Okay?"

"Okay."

Jay turned his head and found Caleb quietly watching him. He smiled at his old friend. "Great concert."

"It doesn't get any better than what we just heard," Caleb said in agreement. "I hear you've been looking for me."

Jay's smile broadened. "I figured you gave the okay to your people to let me know you'd be here tonight. Otherwise I would still be looking for you."

"When legends deign to perform, I try to show up. I thought you might enjoy it too." Caleb's wave of his hand took in the stadium. "Besides, it's a great place to think."

Jay nodded toward Caleb's notebook filled with drawings and calculations. "So I see. Anything?"

"Maybe. We'll see." He looked away. "Great night, isn't it?"

The comment on the night wasn't so much small talk as it was a sign that Caleb's mind had begun to wander. Jay knew his window of opportunity was closing. "Do you remember our last year of school when we were working in the lab together on the same project?"

Caleb's head swung back. "Sure. My design didn't work out. Yours did."

Jay fished the injunction out of the inside pocket of his jacket and handed it to him. "Look at this and tell me if that isn't your patent they're trying to hang me with."

Caleb quickly scanned the document, then handed it back to Jay. "Sure is. It's already been disproved. It's totally bogus."

Relieved, Jay exhaled a long breath. "That's what I thought, but I couldn't be sure until I talked to you. And the damnable thing is it could have taken months to disprove in court if I hadn't recognized the patent and then been able to find you. By then my entire operation would have been down the drain, which of course was exactly what the bastards were counting on." He grimaced. "Will you testify?"

"I'd be happy to. Just tell me when and where." For the first time Caleb looked past Jay to Emily. "Is she your girlfriend?"

Emily, who had been watching and listening to the exchange with fascination, blinked. She had thought Jay's gaze could be intense, but when Caleb focused, his blue eyes were positively laser quality.

"I'm sorry," Jay said. "I should have introduced you two sooner. Emily, this is Caleb McClintock. Caleb, this is Emily Stanton, the woman I love and hope to marry one day soon."

Panic and fear threatened to engulf Emily at Jay's nonchalant words.

Marriage. A living death. What was the difference?

She forced a smile to her face with Caleb. "Hello."

"Hi. This is Daisy." He pointed offhandedly to the redhead beside him, who smiled and didn't seem the least bit offended that Caleb hadn't looked at her in the last two and a half hours. "Are you and Jay going to stay and see Elton John?"

She had actually thought she might want to, but then she had heard Jay introduce her as the woman he loved and hoped to marry and she had remembered. . . . This time tomorrow night she wouldn't be with Jay. She couldn't. Suddenly she wanted to be with him someplace where there weren't thousands of other people. She turned to Jay. "I've decided I'd like to go back to Dallas."

He nodded. "Then that's what we'll do." He rose to his feet and extended his hand to Caleb. "Thanks. I'll let you know the date."

"Do that," Caleb said absently, the pen he held already moving across a clean page of his notebook.

Emily and Jay made love in the jet as it flew through the night toward Texas. To Emily their lovemaking seemed hotter and more intense than ever before. Jay didn't mention love again, but he was unrelenting as he pounded his body into hers. And their joint cries of ecstasy when they climaxed drowned out the sound of the plane's engine.

By the time the wheels of the jet touched down in Dallas, her skin was covered with sweat and her whole body was quivering with exhaustion. And complete physical satisfaction.

She didn't argue with him when he drove to his house

instead of her apartment. She couldn't. She didn't have the strength.

But when she curled her body next to his in bed, she felt a deep, poignant sadness. This would be the last time. The last time . . .

She awoke at dawn when the first fingers of gray light pushed their way into the room. Jay was still asleep beside her, and the sight of him made her heart swell with an unnameable emotion.

Even asleep, Jay had the power to move her, to make her want what she couldn't have, need what was not good for her.

If only he hadn't fallen in love with her, they might have been able to go on together for a while.

With a heavy heart she slipped from the bed and dressed for work in a pair of jeans and a clean white shirt. Then she packed the clothes she had brought with her for the weekend and left the room, heading for the staircase. But when she neared the stairway that led up to the third floor, she slowed, then stopped and looked up. On an impulse she put her bag down and climbed the stairs.

It was a studio, a *sculptor's* studio. It was *Jay's* studio.

She wasn't sure what she had expected, but it certainly wasn't this. As she moved around the studio, she saw that he worked with clay, and must have the forms cast in bronze or some other metal elsewhere. And he always sculpted children; at least that was all she saw.

She remembered the head of the little boy. He had said it was the little boy's expression of happiness that had attracted him. At the time she had simply assumed he was talking about the piece of sculpture. Now she realized he had been talking about the child himself. Jay had probably seen him in a park or on the street and either remembered him or photographed him so that he could sculpt the head and capture the child's expression of joy forever. And then there was the little girl with her nose buried in a flower.

Jay was a gifted, sensitive man. On a certain level she supposed she had always known it. And because he could match her, unhappy experience for unhappy experience, he understood so many things she had previously thought only she knew about.

Was it possible he would also be able to understand her fear of love?

The question continued to haunt her during the day while she worked. The flower arrangements she created veered toward the disordered and turbulent, mirroring how she was feeling on the inside. Harriet gazed at them, bemused, then slapped a high price tag on them. Within hours each arrangement had sold.

Emily barely noticed the activity around her. She couldn't get Jay out of her mind. She pictured him waking up alone and finding her gone this morning, and she wondered what he had thought and felt. She heard his voice, telling her how he had never felt he belonged when he was growing up. She remembered the pieces of sculpture he had done and the patience and depth of emotion that had gone into each work.

He was an extraordinary man, who had never been anything but gentle with her, except in passion, when he had given her the greatest pleasure she had ever known. Would he be able to understand if she told him about her life?

As the day passed, she found herself glancing at her watch every few minutes. Her nerves jumped each time the phone rang or the door chimes sounded, indicating a customer had walked in. She visited her mother during her lunch hour, but was back at work by one. And still Jay didn't come or call.

After all that had been said and done between them, was leaving him going to be as easy as this? she wondered. As calm and as civilized as this? As excruciatingly awful as the pain she felt every time her heart beat?

That evening after work, she arrived home to find an apartment that seemed incredibly empty and a refrigerator with no food. She was just trying to decide if she really wanted to put forth the effort to go out to the grocery store when a knock sounded on her front door.

"What are you doing here?" she asked, instantly catching fire at the sight of Jay. He was dressed conservatively in a dark-brown business suit, pristine white shirt, and designer tie, but there was a look about him that was not quite civilized. Adding to that impression, his eyes were glittering dangerously.

"Did you really think I wouldn't come?" he asked, pushing past her into the small living room.

No, she thought, gazing after him. Somehow she had known he would.

"Why did you leave this morning without waking me up and letting me know?" he asked, rubbing the back of his neck.

"Why haven't you come over or called before now to find out?" She couldn't believe what she had just said. In that one sentence she had effectively told him that she had spent her day wondering why she hadn't heard from him.

He went still. "I spent the day with my lawyers. We have to answer that injunction. If you'd thought, you would have remembered. What are you doing, Emily? Playing some kind of game?"

"I'm sorry. I spoke incorrectly." She waved her hand in front of her as if it would erase the words. "The reason I left without waking you is because I think it's best if we don't see each other again."

"Best for whom?" he asked in an ominously quiet voice.

She turned away from him, unable to continue looking at him. "I know you don't understand—"

He put his hands on her arms and whirled her around. "How can I when you haven't tried to explain?"

She swallowed against a dry throat. "I told you, I don't want you to love me."

"Tough, Emily. I do love you. So deal with it, because I'm not going anywhere."

A sigh shuddered through her body. What was she going to do? she thought dazedly. He was a force she couldn't seem to fight. "Jay . . . love frightens me."

"Why?"

To tell him everything would be the equivalent of scraping her insides. She would be left raw, bleeding, and hurting. And alone. Very alone. Because he wouldn't understand. He couldn't.

The phone rang, and she jumped at the sound. She rarely got phone calls.

Jay muttered an oath. "Let it ring."

"I-I can't. It might be important." She made her way into the kitchen and lifted the phone to her ear. "Hello?"

"Emily, this is Mrs. Thompson."

She straightened. "Has something happened to Mother?"

"No, no, nothing like that. In fact her doctor and physical therapist are very happy with her progress."

"Then what is it?"

"You had asked me to contact you if your mother had any visitors, and a gentleman came to see her a few minutes ago. He said he's a friend of your family."

Ice trickled down her spine. "What's his name?"

"Ralph Llewelyn. He seems extremely nice—"

"I'll be right over, Mrs. Thompson. And, please, until I get there, do not leave him alone with her." She slammed down the receiver and blindly turned.

"What's wrong," Jay asked.

She glanced wildly around for her car keys. "I've got to go see my mother."

"I'll take you."

"No!"

"Yes." He was blocking her way, the embodiment of implacability.

She wanted him with her, she suddenly realized. No longer was she a little girl, staying still so that Ralph wouldn't turn his wrath on her. She was strong and filled with enough anger to face Ralph alone. But she didn't want to be alone. She wanted Jay with her.

And if she turned around after it was all over and he was still there, then maybe for the first time in her life she would be convinced that love was safe. "Let's go."

TEN

Everything seemed normal when they reached the nursing home, but Emily knew better. Ralph's big blue pickup truck sat in the parking lot. The man was predictable in many ways. Year after year he had bought the same size and make of truck in the darkest shade of blue carried. The bigger the truck, Ralph had always believed, the bigger the man. And the windows always stayed down because he considered air conditioning and heaters for sissies.

She hurried into the building and down the hall, and Jay followed silently. Passing the recreational room, she saw Elizabeth playing bridge with three other women. *Dear Lord, don't let my mother be alone with that man.*

When she entered the room, she saw her mother lying in bed, and Ralph, sitting beside her, holding her hand, a pleasant expression on his face. Her mother looked absolutely terrified, and Mrs. Thompson was nowhere to be seen.

"Hello, Emily," Ralph said. "How nice to see you again."

The old fear of him assaulted her, coming at her in waves. She clenched her teeth and fought against the nausea and the all-too-familiar urge to retreat to the stillness within herself. With the fear always came a red haze that blurred her vision. From experience she knew that the red haze could choke her until she couldn't breathe, could blind her until she couldn't see. But today she couldn't let the red haze win. Today she had to conquer it. She kept her gaze steadfastly fixed on her mother's face, and slowly but surely the haze dissipated. "Get away from her, Ralph."

His pleasant expression stayed firmly in place. "I was just telling your mother how much I've missed you since you moved out of the house." He nodded at a point behind her—at Jay, she realized. "She moved out of the house as soon as she graduated from high school, and after that she never even came to visit."

His congenial manner indicated he might be at a church social. He had always excelled at pretense, making the community think he was a devoted husband and father. It had to stop, she thought. The pretense, the lies, the never-ending violence—it all had to stop *now*.

Fury slowly rose in her. Fury for all the times she had seen him smile, then almost casually backhand her mother, sending her flying across the room. Fury for all the times her mother had implored her to lock herself in her room and not come out until she told her it was safe. Fury for all the times she had done as her mother had asked. Fury for all the pain she knew her mother had suffered. Fury for all the tears she had cried. Fury for the way this one man had contaminated every aspect of her life.

Before she knew it, she was at her mother's side, on the opposite side of the bed from him, wrenching her mother's hand from his.

"Emily . . ."

At the sound of her mother's distress, she patted her hand reassuringly, but she never once took her eyes off Ralph. "I visited my mother whenever you weren't around. You didn't know that, did you? And I tried as hard as I could to get her to leave you."

His smile slipped a fraction. "I knew, but I also knew she would never leave me." He stood up and adjusted the waistband of his slacks. "As a matter of fact, it's time for her to come home with me now."

"Over my dead body." If her words had been knives, Ralph would have been bleeding.

His eyes shifted to Jay, who was standing quietly by the door. It was as if he couldn't quite figure out his part in what was happening. Apparently reassured by Jay's continued silence, he quickly sliced his gaze back to her. "You can't separate a man and his wife, Emily, even though God knows you tried often enough when you were growing up. I knew what was going on," he said, again talking to Jay, his tone confiding as if he were talking to a buddy. "I worked hard to give them both a good home, but Emily always hated me because I wasn't her father."

"I *hated* you because you were beating the hell out of my mother every time the least little thing displeased you."

"Now, Emily," he said in a soothing voice that in the past had had the power to make her throw up. Even now she had to fight hard against the nausea rolling in her stomach. "You know that's not true. I was nothing but good to you and your mother. In fact if it hadn't been for me, you would have both been out on the streets, homeless and hungry."

"If it hadn't been for you, you son of a bitch, my mother would be able to walk right now. But instead you beat her and threw her down the stairs and then went out for a night of drinking, leaving her unconscious and bleeding on the floor. If it hadn't been for the next-door neighbor coming by the next morning and finding her, she'd be dead now."

She moved toward him, wanting to be close enough to him so that she could physically hurt him as he had so often hurt her mother. She wanted to scream at the top of her lungs at him to match the screaming she had heard in her head for years. "But Mother was still too afraid of you to press charges, and the police had no evidence that it was you who assaulted her. You, of course, had taken the precaution of smashing a back window so that it would look like a break-in, and once again you and your friends were able to come up with a bogus alibi for you. Tell me, Ralph, why has she stayed afraid of you all these years? What hold do you have over her? You must have something. It's the only thing that makes any sense."

"Emily," her mother said, her voice weak and agitated, "leave it alone."

"Listen to your mother, little girl. You've done enough, taking her out of the hospital in Houston and spiriting her up here so that I couldn't find her for all these months. I've spent every weekend since looking for you two." His eyes flicked back to Jay, and dawning recognition drew a broad smile from him. "It was just luck that I happened to be looking in a Dallas paper one day and saw that picture of you. Fortunately since Mr. Barrett has such a high profile in the area, it was fairly easy to find out where he lived. All I had to do was stake out the place, and when you left this morning, I followed you to work and then here." He paused. "You looked real pretty in that picture. I was just telling your mother it would be a shame for that pretty face of yours to get rearranged."

She sensed more than saw Jay jerk. She held up her hand to him. This was her fight, and she was determined to see it through. "You don't scare me, Ralph. Not any more. If you don't get out of here, I'm going to call the police."

He smiled again, but it wasn't a pleasant smile.

"Sure thing, honey. I'll leave, but I'm taking my wife with me." He turned and jerked open a drawer of a nearby chest. "Is this your stuff, Mary?"

"I'm sorry, but I had to take a phone call," Mrs. Thompson said, walking briskly in. "I didn't think it would take as long as it did. . . ." Her voice faded away as she scanned the room. "What's going on here?"

"Please call the police, Mrs. Thompson. I want this man escorted from the premises, and I will do whatever needs to be done to see that he's not allowed near my mother again."

Ralph's jaw squared. "Mary is my wife. I'm taking her home."

Emily opened her mouth, but her mother spoke first. "No. I'm not going with you, Ralph." Her hands shook on top of the coverlet, but her voice was stronger than it had been before. Emily moved back to her side and took her hand. "I stayed with you for years because you said if I didn't, you'd hurt Emily."

So there it was, Emily thought, tears filling her eyes until she couldn't see. *She* had been the weapon Ralph had used against her mother. All these years, her mother had been so afraid for her that she had done the only thing she could think of to protect her—take the beating for her. What agony she must have gone through, fearing for both of them.

Her mother was continuing. "But you've threatened my child and me for the last time. Emily has worked hard to make us a new life, and from this point forward

I'm going to help her. As soon as I can, I'm going to divorce you, and if you contest it, I'll tell the police everything."

Ralph's big hands bunched into fists. Emily tensed, physically preparing to protect her mother. . . But she had forgotten about Jay.

He moved away from the door and crossed the room to the foot of the bed. His position put him between her and Ralph. Though slimmer than Ralph, he was several inches taller and in obviously good physical condition. He looked every bit the dangerous man she had first pegged him to be, but for a different reason.

She had been afraid of him then because she had instinctively known he had the power to make her fall in love with him. But now she saw him as Ralph must be seeing him. Granite hard and frighteningly calm, with an icy menace in his eyes that she had never seen before. In short he looked like nothing less than a lethal weapon. Apparently Ralph made the same judgment, because Emily saw his hands relax.

"I hadn't realized until today what was going on," Jay said in a conversational tone that, by its very mildness, chilled. "But now that I do, I want you to know that if you ever come near either of these two women again, I will take great pleasure in personally killing you."

Ralph visibly paled. "You don't scare me," he blustered. "Just because you have more money than God doesn't give you the right to threaten a person." He pointed at an obviously upset Mrs. Thompson. "You heard him. You're my witness. If he does anything to me, I want you to call the police."

It took Emily a moment to realize that Ralph was scared, and when she did realize it, she almost let out a whoop of joy.

As if he sensed her inner glee, he fixed a hate-filled gaze on her, but he began edging toward the door. "You and your mother haven't seen the last of me! Don't for a minute think you have!" He sent his wife a glance that was obviously supposed to carry meaning, and then he was gone.

His threats had sounded empty, even to Emily. In the time-honored manner of a bully, he had retreated when he had sensed superior odds. With a cry of relief she sank onto the bed and hugged her mother's frail body to her. "It's over, Mom. It's finally over. We're going to be all right."

So now he understood why he had sensed a firsthand knowledge of sin in Emily, Jay thought as he sat quietly in a corner of the room, watching her stroke her mother's hair. A doctor had seen Mary and sedated her. It was only a matter of time before she fell asleep.

Since Ralph had departed, Jay had left the room only once, stepping into the hall to speak to Mrs. Thompson about his hiring a security guard for Mary. She had agreed. By midnight there would be a guard at Mary's door. She would be taken care of.

But it was Emily he was worried about.

He understood so much now. While still small and defenseless, she had learned about violence in a way no one should, much less a child. It wasn't any wonder she was so guarded, and it was no less amazing that love frightened her. She had called it a trap, and after listening to her, her mother, and her stepfather, he knew why.

It presented him with a huge problem. He didn't want her to feel trapped, but he couldn't let her go either.

Emily cast one last look at her mother's sleeping form before she left. She stopped for a moment in the recreation room and spoke a few quiet words to Elizabeth. When she came back out into the hall, Jay was waiting for her and was right beside her when she walked outside into the darkness.

The nursing home was on a hill, and the lights of the city could be seen in the distance. But where they were, at the edge of the parking lot, there was very little light.

She was glad. Rationally or irrationally, she felt as if in the last few hours she had been exposed to a barrage of unbearably bright light. It was as if her life had been split wide open and all the dark corners had been exposed. It had been long overdue, and she had been left exhausted. She felt as if she could sleep forever.

But before she did . . .

In the middle of the parking lot she slowed to a halt and reached out a hand to Jay so that he stopped too.

For a moment she was at a loss for words. Finally she simply said, "You stayed."

"Did you really think I would leave you?"

Dark shadows contoured his face, making him appear sinister, but she wasn't afraid of him. He now knew the worst about her, and she didn't plan to hide anything from him anymore. "I wasn't sure, but I'm glad you didn't. I'm glad you know."

"I am too. I just wish you'd told me sooner."

His voice sounded comforting in the darkness, deep and strong. "I couldn't. I've never talked to anyone about it. It was too hard."

"I understand. There haven't been too many people I've been able to talk to about my childhood either."

"My guess is you put everything into your sculptures, just as I put a lot of my emotions into my flower arrangements."

His brows rose in surprise. "You know about my sculpting?"

"I went up there this morning and saw all your happy children. You're very talented."

"Thank you." He smiled. "I guess a psychologist would say that I've found an outlet to balance what I went through. All I know is that sculpting children makes me feel good. I suppose it's an affirmation for me that there really is happiness." He smiled and brushed a hand over her cheek. "Sort of like believing there are stars, even when you can't see them."

She shook her head. "I still am not sure they're there unless I can see them."

"Then you still don't trust. What about me? Do you trust me enough to accept me and love me?"

"Try to see it the way I do, Jay. It's not you I don't trust. It's . . . everything else." She wrapped her arms around her waist, hugging herself.

"Come home with me."

"I can't. I'm exhausted."

"Come home with me and let me hold you while you sleep."

She sighed. "I don't know—"

All at once they were caught in the harsh glare of headlights. Confused, Emily lifted her hand to shield her eyes and found herself staring straight at a big, familiar truck. "Oh, God, it's Ralph."

Immobilized, she listened as he gunned the motor. He wouldn't go up against Jay alone, but having a three-quarter-ton pickup truck as a weapon had brought back his courage. And now he was going to kill them.

Tires squealed in a high, tortured scream as he floored the accelerator pedal. Jay gave Emily a hard shove sideways, and for her it seemed that time slowed to a crawl. She staggered, taking several steps to her right as she fought for balance. She tripped over a curb and fell into a flower bed that was bordered with large rocks, and landed on one knee. Pain. It shot through her as the sharp edges of a rock bit into the soft flesh of her palm, but she felt it only peripherally.

In that precise moment Jay was at the center of everything for her. Why wasn't he *moving*? He was just standing there, looking at her. And Ralph had the truck aimed straight at him, like a high-powered bullet that in the next half second was going to make impact with his body.

Frantic, half out of her mind, she acted instinctively, using the only weapon at her disposal. She grabbed the rock and stood. As the truck drew even with her, she hurled the rock as hard as she could.

She heard it smash the windshield and skid across the hood. At the same time she heard a sharp cry of surprise from Ralph, saw him jerk the wheel, then the back end of the truck fishtail. Veering wildly to the left away from Jay, the truck jumped a curb, hurtled downhill out of control, and slammed sideways into a corner of a building, the driver side crumpling inward.

There was a crash, the sound of crunching metal and shattering glass, and then silence.

And then she heard herself scream.

"*Jay? Jay?*"

She saw him then, about six feet away, pushing up from the ground where he had landed after leaping aside at the last possible moment.

"Stay here," he ordered, and ran down the hill to

the truck. After a minute he returned, his face grim. "He's unconscious, and he looks badly hurt. But whatever happens, Emily, you and your mother will never have to worry about him again." He tried to draw her against him, but she resisted. Her body was absolutely rigid, her gaze was riveted on the truck. "The accident wasn't your fault," he said softly. "He did himself in with his own hatred and anger. He was going way too fast to ever have been able to control the truck." He hesitated, studying her with concern. "We're going to have to wait and talk to the police. Are you up to it?"

"Of course," she said dully. "I'm fine."

Emily answered all the police's questions mechanically. Then without bothering to ask her permission, Jay took her to his house and put her to bed.

She slept deeply, and while she did, he watched over her, leaving the bedroom only when his attorneys called. A court date for the patent-infringement lawsuit had been set for the following week, and Caleb's office had also been notified. Jay had no doubt Caleb would show up. He had a way of remembering what was truly important.

Downstairs Roberta was cooking up a storm. It didn't matter that they both knew Emily would never be able to eat half the amount she was preparing. Cooking was Roberta's way of caring, and to Jay's mind Emily deserved all the nurturing she could get.

Around sundown of the next day Emily finally stirred awake. When she opened her eyes, the first thing she saw was Jay, sprawled in an easy chair beside the bed, asleep.

A scene flashed into her mind, a nightmarish memory of Ralph's truck hurtling toward Jay and how he had stayed firmly planted where he was until the last possible second, providing Ralph a target so that she would be safe. In that instant when she had thought he was going to be killed, she had looked at him and felt as if she were looking straight into the center of her heart.

She loved him. And he loved her.

Because of her he had almost died. And after the ugliness of the night she had looked around and he had still been there beside her. Yes, he loved her.

It was so simple. So complicated.

She slipped from the bed and went to take a shower. She tried to keep her bandaged hand dry, but soon gave up. The bandage, she remembered, had been Jay's idea. He had been concerned about protecting her hand where the skin had been scraped off.

After she toweled off, she dressed in a pair of her jeans and a T-shirt that had been, she discovered, freshly laundered, and then put a new bandage on her hand. When she returned to the bedroom, Jay was awake and waiting for her, looking incredibly vital—the exact opposite of the way she felt.

"I brought up some food," he said, waving his hand toward a table on top of which were a steaming bowl of soup, a pile of sandwiches, and two glasses of iced tea. "I figured you must be starved."

She studied him searchingly. "Are you all right? You couldn't have gotten much rest in that chair."

"Part of the night I was in bed with you."

She remembered now—an impression of being held and protected while she slept.

"Your mother's fine," he said, misinterpreting her silence. "Ralph's condition is another matter. He's in a coma and was operated on last night. It appears his spine has been irreversibly damaged." He waited for her to say something, but she remained silent. "Why don't you come sit down and have something to eat?"

"In a minute." She walked to him and took his hands in hers. "First I want to thank you for all you've done for me."

"I wish I could have done more, and I wish to hell I could have done it sooner."

She shook her head. "You did more than enough. Because of me, you almost lost your life."

He freed a hand so that he could tenderly curve it along her jawline. "There wasn't a chance I would leave you. I love you too much."

Tears sprang to her eyes. "And I love you."

He exhaled an uneven breath, and it sounded like a release of pain. "Really?"

She nodded solemnly. "Really."

"Thank God," he muttered roughly and pulled her into his arms.

A tear slipped from her eye and rolled down her cheek as she pressed her face against his chest and said a silent prayer of thanks for his safety. She could hear his heart beating strongly. If anything had happened to him, she would never have been able to forgive herself. Several more tears slipped from her eyes. She felt so sad, so very tired. . . .

When he felt her tears soaking through his shirt, he held her a little away from him and gazed down at her with concern. "What's wrong, Emily?"

"I can't stay with you, Jay."

"What do you mean? You just told me you loved me."

"I do, but I can't risk any more heartbreak. I just can't. I'm sorry. I'm so sorry." Her tears were flowing more freely now, and she couldn't seem to stop them. She broke away from him and put a hand to her forehead. "I'm so tired, Jay, which is totally stupid, since I've just slept almost eighteen hours straight. But I'm exhausted. I don't have any more strength. Don't you see? I can't risk being with you, loving you day in and day out, and then have that happiness fall apart. I can't let myself trust love. I can't let myself trust happiness."

"Yeah, I see." He took her hand and led her to the couch. Gently he sat her down and then, still holding her hand, dropped down beside her and angled his body so that he was facing her. "You've been running on nerves for God knows how long, Emily. You're emotionally drained. After the life you've led, it's only natural that you don't think feelings like love and happiness and security will last. And I can't promise you that things aren't going to happen that will be beyond your control and beyond my control. But what I *can* promise you is that, if you stay with me and live with me, we'll face whatever happens together, and *together* we'll make it through."

She heard his words, but she couldn't seem to take in their meaning. "You want me to live here with you?"

"I want you to marry me, Emily. I want to spend the rest of my life with you."

She gazed at him without speaking for a long time. As tired and as weak and as confused as she felt at the moment, she knew one thing: There was no way she could leave him. She needed him too much, and loved him beyond anything she had ever thought possible. She still had a great many fears, and she didn't believe that love and happiness would last. But she couldn't risk never seeing Jay again, couldn't risk never knowing the ecstasy of making love with him again, of never waking up and seeing him beside her.

"I won't marry you," she said softly. "But I'll live with you if you like . . . for a while."

He slowly smiled. "I'm going to take your *a while* and turn it into the rest of our lives. You'll see."

One Year Later

Emily stood out on the back terrace, her eyes on her mother as she walked slowly through the garden with the help of a nurse and a walker. Her mother had made amazing progress over the last year. With the specter of Ralph removed from her life, she had found new determination. Even the doctors had been amazed by her grit. As soon as she had been physically able, Jay had moved her into a large downstairs room that overlooked the garden and hired all the medical help she needed and then some. Due to Roberta's cooking she had even gained some much-needed weight.

Emily had been overwhelmed by his generosity to her mother, but then he also overwhelmed her on a daily basis, showering her with love and attention. She had always known how to be afraid, but Jay had taught her about love and trust, not by doing or saying any one thing but with little things, such as a word, a touch, a gesture.

So slowly that she hadn't even noticed it happening, she had begun to heal, until now when she had never felt emotionally stronger or happier.

She kept her eyes on her mother until she disappeared into the rose arbor, then she turned. Jay was there, leaning against the doorjamb, his hands in the pockets of his tailored slacks.

"Hi, I didn't know you were home."

He wondered if she was aware of how easily she referred to his home as hers these days. He wondered if she knew how beautiful she looked against the backdrop of the garden with the sunlight in her hair and on her skin and all signs of strain gone from her face. He wondered if she knew how happy she had made him. "I just arrived."

"I'm glad because I have something to tell you."

"I'm listening."

She had never seen him look more handsome or compelling, she thought, her heart turning over with love. This last year with him had been an amazing adventure full of laughter, tenderness, and passion. And now there was another adventure in front of her:

"I'm pregnant, Jay."

A smile began to spread across his face, and it didn't stop until he looked as if he was lit from the inside out with joy. But he didn't move. "That's wonderful."

She gripped her hands tightly together. "I'm very happy about it."

His gaze dropped to her hands, then returned to her face. "And I'm ecstatic, but you know that, don't you?"

"Yes."

He looked at her for a long moment. "Tell me what you want, Emily."

She listened very carefully to the question and thought about it. He had asked her the question before, and he had always given her what she had asked for. So why was she feeling anxious? she asked herself. Why was she feeling troubled?

Because of Jay she knew about love and trust. Because of Jay she knew that she would never be alone when fear came, that he would always be with her to help her deal with the bad times and rejoice with her in the good times.

"Emily?"

Suddenly, finally, it was all so simple, she thought, gazing at him. In fact she was bewildered that she had ever thought otherwise.

She graced Jay with a full, bright smile. At last she knew *exactly* what it was that she wanted. "I want to marry you, have babies for us to love, build a family to fill all our homes, and spend the rest of my life with you."

He didn't appear to move, but all at once she was in his arms. "Don't ever expect me to let you go," he murmured, his voice choked with emotion. He lowered his head to kiss her, and he didn't stop for a long, long time.

THE EDITOR'S CORNER

July belongs to ONLY DADDY—and six magnificent heroes who discover romance, family style! Whether he's a confirmed bachelor or a single father, a small-town farmer or a big-city cop, each of these men can't resist the pitter-patter of little feet. And when he falls under the spell of that special woman's charms, he'll stop at nothing to claim her as a partner in parenting and passion. . . .

Leading the terrific line-up for July is Linda Cajio with **ME AND MRS. JONES**, LOVESWEPT #624. Actually, it should be *ex*-Mrs. Jones since high school sweethearts Kate Perry and Mitch Jones have been divorced for eleven years, after an elopement and a disastrous brief marriage. Now Kate is back in town, and Mitch, who's always been able to talk her into just about anything, persuades her to adopt a wise-eyed injured tomcat, with the promise that he'd be making plenty of house calls! Not sure she can play stepmother to his daughter Chelsea, Kate tells herself to run from the man who so easily ignites her desire, but she still remembers his hands on her body and can't send him away. To Mitch, no memory can ever match the heat of their passion, and he's been waiting all this time to reclaim the only woman he's ever truly loved. With fire in his touch, he sets about convincing her to let him in once more, and this time he intends to keep her in his arms for always. An utterly delightful story from beginning to end, told with Linda's delicious sense of humor and sensitive touch.

In **RAISING HARRY**, LOVESWEPT #625 by Victoria Leigh, Griff Ross is a single father coping with the usual problems of raising a high-spirited three-year-old son. He's never been jealous of Harry until he finds him in the arms of their neighbor Sharron Capwell. Her lush mouth makes Griff long to kiss her breathless, while her soft curves tempt him with visions of bare shoulders touched only by moonlight and his hands. She makes him burn with pleasure as no woman ever has, but Griff, still hurt by a betrayal he's never forgiven, insists he wants only a friend and a lover. Single and childless, Sharron has always been content with her life—until she thrills to the ecstacy Griff shows her, and now finds herself struggling with her need to be his wife and Harry's mother. Rest assured that a happily-ever-after awaits these two, as well as the young one, once they admit the love they can't deny. Victoria tells a compelling love story, one you won't be able to put down.

Who can resist **THE COURTING COWBOY**, LOVESWEPT #626 by Glenna McReynolds? Ty Garrett is a rough-edged rancher who wants a woman to share the seasons, to love under the Colorado skies. But he expects that finding a lady in his middle-of-nowhere town would be very rough—until a spirited visiting teacher fascinates his son and captivates him too! Victoria Willoughby has beautiful skin, a very kissable mouth, and a sensual innocence that beckons Ty to woo her with fierce, possessive passion. He awakens her to pleasures she's never imagined, teaches her how wonderful taking chances can be, and makes her feel alluring, wanton. But she's already let one man rule her life and she's vowed never to belong to anyone ever again. Still, she knows that finding Ty is a miracle; now if she'll only realize that he's the best man and the right man for her . . . Glenna's talent shines brightly in this terrific romance.

Bonnie Pega begins her deliciously sexy novel, **THEN COMES MARRIAGE**, LOVESWEPT #627, with the hero and heroine meeting in a very unlikely place. Single mother-to-be Libby Austin certainly thinks that seeing the hunk of her dreams in a childbirth class is truly rotten luck, but she breathes a sigh of relief when she discovers that Zac Webster is coaching his sister-in-law, not his wife! His potent masculinity can charm every stitch of clothing off a woman's body; too bad he makes it all too clear that a child doesn't fit into his life. Still, unable to resist the temptation of Libby's blue velvet eyes and delectable smile, Zac lays siege to her senses, and her response of torrential kisses and fevered caresses drive him even wilder with hunger. Libby has given him more than he's hoped for—and a tricky dilemma. Can a man who's sworn off marriage and vows he's awful with kids claim a wildfire bride and her baby? With this wonderful romance, her second LOVESWEPT, Bonnie proves that she's a name to watch for.

There's no sexier **MAN AROUND THE HOUSE** than the hero in Cindy Gerard's upcoming LOVESWEPT, #628. Matthew Spencer is a lean, muscled heartbreaker, and when he answers his new next-door neighbor's cries for help, he finds himself rescuing disaster-prone Katie

McDonald, who's an accident waiting to happen—and a sassy temptress who's sure to keep him up nights. Awakening his hunger with the speed of a summer storm, Katie senses his pain and longs to comfort him, but Matthew makes her feel too much, makes her want more than she can have. Though she lets herself dare to dream of being loved, Katie knows she's all wrong for a man who's walking a careful path to regain custody of his son. He needs nice and normal, not her kind of wild and reckless—no matter that they sizzle in each other's arms. But Matthew's not about to give up a woman who adores his child, listens to his favorite golden oldie rock station, and gives him kisses that knock his socks off and make the stars spin. The magic of Cindy's writing shines through in this enchanting tale of love.

Finishing the line-up in a big way is Marcia Evanick and **IN DADDY'S ARMS,** LOVESWEPT #629. Brave enough to fight back from wounds inflicted in the line of duty, Bain O'Neill is devastated when doctors tell him he'll never be a father. Having a family is the only dream that ever mattered to him, a fantasy he can't give up, not when he knows that somewhere there are two children who are partly his, the result of an anonymous sperm donation he made years ago. A little investigation helps him locate his daughters—and their mother, Erin Flynn, a fiery-haired angel who tastes as good as she looks. Widowed for two years, Erin takes his breath away and heals him with her loving touch. Bain hates keeping the truth from her, and though the children soon beg him to be their daddy, he doesn't dare confess his secret to Erin, not until he's silenced her doubts about his love and makes her believe he's with her to stay forever. All the stirring emotions and funny touches that you've come to expect from Marcia are in this fabulous story.

On sale this month from Bantam are three spectacular women's novels. Dianne Edouard and Sandra Ware have teamed up once again and written **SACRED LIES,** a spellbinding novel of sin, seduction, and betrayal. Romany Chase is the perfect spy: intelligent, beautiful, a woman who thrills to the hunt. But with her latest mission, Romany is out of her depth. Adrift in a world where redemption may arrive too late, she is torn between the enigmatic priest she has orders to seduce and the fierce agent she desires. Beneath the glittering Roman moon, a deadly conspiracy of greed, corruption, and shattering evil is closing in, and Romany must choose whom to believe—and whom to love.

With more than several million copies of her novels in print, Kay Hooper is indisputably one of the best loved and popular authors of romantic fiction—and now she has penned **THE WIZARD OF SEATTLE,** a fabulous, magical story of immortal love and mesmerizing fantasy. Serena Smyth travels cross-country to Seattle to find Richard Patrick Merlin, guided by an instinct born of her determination to become a master wizard like him. She knows he can be her teacher, but she never expects the fire he ignites in her body and soul. Their love forbidden by an ancient law, Serena and Merlin will take a desperate gamble and travel to the long-lost world of Atlantis—to change the history that threatens to keep them apart for eternity.

From bestselling author Susan Johnson comes **SILVER FLAME,** the steamy sequel about the Braddock-Black dynasty you read about in **BLAZE.** Pick up a copy and find out why *Romantic Times* gave the author its Best Sensual Historical Romance Award. Sizzling with electrifying sensuality, **SILVER FLAME** burns hot! When Empress

Jordan is forced to sell her most precious possession to the highest bidder in order to feed her brothers and sisters, Trey Braddock-Black knows he must have her, no matter what the cost. The half-Absarokee rogue has no intention of settling down with one woman, but once he's spent three weeks with the sweet enchantress, he knows he can never give her up. . . .

Also on sale this month, in the hardcover edition from Doubleday, is **THE PAINTED LADY,** the stunningly sensual debut novel by Lucia Grahame. All of Paris and London recognize Fleur not only as Frederick Brooks's wife, but also as the successful painter's most inspiring model. But few know the secrets behind his untimely death and the terrible betrayal that leaves Fleur with a heart of ice—and no choice but to accept Sir Anthony Camwell's stunning offer: a fortune to live on in return for five nights of unrestrained surrender to what he plans to teach her—the exquisite art of love.

Happy reading!

With warmest wishes,

Nita Taublib

Nita Taublib
Associate Publisher
LOVESWEPT and FANFARE

Don't miss these exciting
books by your favorite
Bantam authors
On Sale in May:

SACRED LIES
by Dianne Edouard
and Sandra Ware

THE WIZARD OF SEATTLE
by Kay Hooper

SILVER FLAME
by Susan Johnson

"SPECIAL SNEAK PREVIEW"
THE MAGNIFICENT ROGUE
by Iris Johansen
On Sale in August

SACRED LIES
by Dianne Edouard and Sandra Ware

On Sale in May

Romany Chase is the perfect spy: intelligent, beautiful, a woman who thrills to the hunt. But torn between the fierce Israeli agent she desires and the enigmatic priest she has orders to seduce, Romany is out of her depth—adrift in a world where redemption may arrive too late . . . .

As soon as Romany opened the door, she knew she wasn't alone. Someone waited for her. Somewhere in the apartment.

She had never carried a gun. There had never been a need. Even though Sully could have gotten her easy clearance, and had more than once urged her to take along some insurance. But her assignments never warranted it. Except that one time, in Geneva, and that situation had come totally out of left field.

She allowed her eyes to become adjusted to the gloom and, easing herself against the wall, moved to the edge of the living room. She searched the shadows. Strained to see something behind the thick lumps and bumps of furniture. Nothing. She crouched lower and inched closer to the door opening into her bedroom.

She peered around the corner. Whoever was in the apartment had switched on the ceiling fan and the small lamp that sat on a dressing table in the adjoining bath. The soft light cast the room in semidarkness, and she could make out the large solid shape of a man. He reclined easily upon her bed, a marshmallowy heap of pillows propped against his back. He hadn't bothered to draw back the covers, and he lay on top of the spread completely naked.

She should have run, gotten out of her apartment as quickly as possible. Except she recognized the hard muscles under the deeply tanned skin, the black curling hair, the famous smirk that passed for a smile. Recognized the man who was a cold-blooded killer—and her lover.

Romany moved through the doorway and smiled. "I'm not even going to ask how you got in here, David."

She heard his dark laugh. "Is that any way to greet an old friend?"

She walked farther into the room and stood by the side of the bed. She stared into the bright green eyes, still a surprise after all this time. But then everything about David ben Haar was a surprise. "Why don't you make yourself comfortable?"

"I am . . . almost." He reached for her hand and ran it slowly down his chest, stopping just short of the black hair at his groin.

She glanced down, focusing on her hand, pale and thin clasped inside his. She could hear her breath catch inside her throat. And as if that sound had been meant as some sort of signal, he pulled her down beside him.

She rested with her back against him, letting him work the muscles at her shoulders, brush his lips against her hair. She didn't turn when she finally decided to speak. "What are you doing here, David?"

"I came to see you." The words didn't sound like a complete lie.

She twisted herself round to look up at him. "That's terribly flattering, David, but it won't work."

She watched the smirk almost stretch into a real smile.

"Okay, I came to make sure that Sully is taking good care of my girl."

"I'm not your girl, David." She tried not to sound mean, or hurt, or anything. But she could feel the muscles of his stomach tighten against her back.

"You know Sully's a fucking asshole," he said finally. "What's he waiting on, those jerks to open up a concentration camp and gas a few thousand Jews?"

"David, Sully's not an asshole. . . . Hey, what in the hell do you mean?" She jerked around, waiting for an answer, watching his eyes turn cold.

"Gimme a break, Romany."

"Dammit, David, I don't have the slightest idea what you're talking about. Besides, what in the hell have concentration camps got to do with . . . ?" She stopped short, not willing to play her hand, even though David probably knew all the cards she was holding.

"Well, Romany, I can save you, and Sully, and all your little friends over at the CIA a whole helluva lotta trouble. Somebody—and I think you're deaf, dumb, and blind if you haven't pegged who that is—is stealing the Church blind, swiping paintings right off the museum walls, then slipping by some pretty goddamn good fakes."

She watched him stare at her from inside the darkness of her bed, waiting with that flirting smirk on his mouth for her to say something. But she didn't answer.

" . . . And the SOB at the other end of this operation"—he was finishing what he'd started—"whether your CIA geniuses want to admit it or not, is black-marketing the genuine articles, funneling the profits to a group of neo-Nazis who aren't going to settle for German reunification."

"Neo-Nazis?"

She could hear him grit his teeth. "Yeah, neo-Nazis. Getting East and West Germany together was just the first stage of their nasty little operation. They've got big plans, Romany. But they're the same old fuckers. Just a little slicker."

"David, I can't believe—"

"Shit, you people never want to believe—"

"Stop it, David."

He dropped his head and took in a deep staccatoed breath. She felt his hands move up her arms to her shoulders and force her body close to his. "Sorry, Romany." He sounded hoarse. Then suddenly she felt him laughing against her. "You know something"— he was drawing back—"you're on the wrong side, Romany. We wouldn't have these stupid fights if you'd come and work with me. With the Mossad."

"Yeah? Work with you, huh? And just what inducement can you offer, David ben Haar?" She pulled away from him and stood up.

Her feelings about David were a tangled mess—which, after she'd watched him board the plane for Tel Aviv thirteen months ago, she'd thought she could safely leave unwound. But here he was again, still looking at her with that quizzical twist to his lips that she couldn't help but read as a challenge.

She wanted his hands on her. That was the thought that kept repeating itself, blotting out everything else in her mind. Her own hands trembled as she pushed the hair away from her neck and began to undo the buttons at her back. Undressing for him slowly, the way he liked it.

She hadn't let herself know how much she'd missed this, until she was beneath the covers naked beside him, and his hands were really on her again, taking control, his mouth moving everywhere on her body. The pulse of the ceiling fan blended suddenly with the rush of blood in her ears, and David's heat was under her skin like fire.

She pressed herself closer against him, her need for him blocking out her doubts. She wanted his solidness, his back under her hands, the hardness of him along the length of her body. David ben Haar, the perfect sexual fantasy. But real. Flesh and blood with eyes green as the sea. She looked into his eyes as he pulled her beneath him. There was no lightness in them now, only the same intensity of passion as when he killed. He came into her hard, and she shut her eyes, matching her rhythm to his. To dream was all right, as long as you didn't let it go beyond the borders of your bed.

*   *   *

With one small edge of the curtain rolled back, David ben Haar could just see through the balcony railing where the red Alfa Romeo Spider was waiting to park in the street. Romany had been flying about the apartment when the car had first driven up, still cursing him for her half-damp hair, amusingly anxious to keep the priest from getting as far as her door.

"I could hide in the bedroom." He had said it from his comfortable position, lying still naked on her sofa. Laughing at her as she went past buttoning her dress, hobbling on one shoe back to the bedroom.

"I don't trust you, David ben Haar." She'd come back with her other shoe and was throwing a hairbrush into that satchel she called a purse.

"Romany?" He had concentrated on the intent face, the wild curls threatening to break loose from the scarf that bound them. "Morrow one of the bad guys?"

Picking up a sweater, she had looked over at him then, with something remarkably like guilt. "I don't know." She was going for the door. "That's what I'm supposed to find out."

Then she was gone, her heels rat-tatting down the stairs. High heels at Villa d'Este. Just like an American. They never took anything seriously, then covered it up with a cynicism they hadn't earned. Romany was the flip side of that, of course, all earnestness and innocence. She was smart and she had guts. But it wouldn't be enough to protect her. He got up.

As he watched now, the Spider was swinging into the parking space that had finally become available at the curb. The door opened and a man got out, turning to where Romany had just emerged from under the balcony overhang. The man didn't exactly match the car, he looked far too American. What he didn't look like was a priest.

He watched them greet each other. Very friendly. The compressor on the air conditioner picked that minute to kick in again, so he couldn't hope to hear what was said. The man opened the passenger door for her, then walked around to get in. They didn't pull out right away, and he was wondering why when he saw the canvas top go down. The engine roared up as they shot away from the curb. He could tell by the tilt of her head that Romany was laughing.

They had not spoken for some time now, standing among the tall cypress, looking out below to the valley. The dying sun had painted everything in a kind of saturated light, and he seemed almost surreal standing next to her, his fair aureole of hair and tall body in light-colored shirt and slacks glowing against the blackness of the trees.

They had played today, she and Julian Morrow. Like happy strangers who had met in Rome, with no history and no future. She had felt it immediately, the playfulness, implicit in the red car, in the way he wore the light, casual clothes. Like an emblem, like a costume at a party.

She had sat in the red car, letting the wind blow everything away from her mind, letting it rip David from her body. Forgetting the job. Forgetting that the man beside her was a priest and a suspect, and she a paid agent of the United States government.

They had played today. And she had liked this uncomplicated persona better than any he had so far let her see. Liked his ease and his sense of humor, and the pleasure he had seemed to find in their joyful sharing of this place. She had to stop playing now, but this was the Julian Morrow she must hold in her mind. Not the priest. Not the suspect in criminal forgery. But a Julian Morrow to whom she could want to make love.

He turned to her and smiled. For a moment the truth of her treachery rose to stick in her throat. But she forced it down. This was her job. She was committed.

She smiled back, moving closer, as if she might want a better view, or perhaps some little shelter from the wind. He must have thought the latter, because she felt his hands draping her sweater more firmly around her shoulders.

Time to take the advantage. And shifting backward, she pressed herself lightly against his chest, her eyes closed. She was barely breathing, feeling for any answering strain. But she could find no sense of any rejection in his posture.

She turned. He was looking down at her. His eyes, so close, were unreadable. She would never remember exactly what had happened next, but she knew when her arms went around him. And the small moment of her triumph when she felt him hard against her. Then she was pulling him down toward her, her fingers tangling in his hair, her mouth moving on his.

At the moment when she ceased thinking at all, he let her go, suddenly, with a gesture almost brutal that set her tumbling back. His hand reached for her wrist, didn't let her fall. But the grip was not kind or gentle.

His face was closed. Completely. Anger would have been better. She was glad when he turned away from her, walking back in the direction of the car. There would be no dinner tonight at the wonderful terraced restaurant he had talked about today. Of that she was perfectly sure. It was going to be a long drive back to Rome.

THE WIZARD OF SEATTLE
the unique new romantic fantasy from
Kay Hooper

On Sale in May

In the bestselling tradition of the time-travel romances of Diana Gabaldon and Constance O'Day-Flannery, Kay Hooper creates her own fabulous, magical story of timeless love and mesmerizing fantasy.

She looked like a ragged, storm-drenched urchin, but from the moment Serena Smyth appeared on his Seattle doorstep Richard Patrick Merlin recognized the spark behind her green eyes, the wild talent barely held in check. And he would help her learn to control her gift, despite a taboo so ancient that the reasons for its existence had been forgotten. But he never suspected that in his rebellion he would risk all he had and all he was to feel a love none of his kind had ever known.

Seattle, 1984

It was his home. She knew that, although where her certainty came from was a mystery to her. Like the inner tug that had drawn her across the country to find him, the knowledge seemed instinctive, beyond words or reason. She didn't even know his name. But she knew what he was. He was what she wanted to be, needed to be, what all her instincts insisted she had to be, and only he could teach her what she needed to learn.

Until this moment, she had never doubted that he would accept her as his pupil. At sixteen, she was passing through that stage of development experienced by humans, twice in their lifetimes, a stage marked by total self-absorption and the unshakable certainty that the entire universe revolves around oneself. It occurred in infancy and in adolescence, but rarely ever again, unless one were utterly unconscious of reality. Those traits had given her the confidence she had needed in order to cross the country alone with no more than a ragged backpack and a few dollars.

But they deserted her now, as she stood at the wrought iron gates and stared up at the secluded old Victorian house. The rain beat down on her, and lightning flashed in the stormy sky, illuminating the turrets and gables of the house; there were few lighted windows, and those were dim rather than welcoming.

It *looked* like the home of a wizard.

She almost ran, abruptly conscious of her aloneness. But then she squared her thin shoulders, shoved open the gate, and walked steadily to the front door. Ignoring the bell, she used the brass knocker to rap sharply. The knocker was fashioned in the shape of an owl, the creature that symbolized wisdom, a familiar of wizards throughout fiction.

She didn't know about fact.

Her hand was shaking, and she gave it a fierce frown as she rapped the knocker once more against the solid door. She barely had time to release the knocker before the door was pulled open.

Tall and physically powerful, his raven hair a little shaggy and his black eyes burning with an inner fire, he surveyed the dripping, ragged girl on his doorstep with lofty disdain for long moments during which all of her determination melted away to nothing. Then he caught her collar with one elegant hand, much as he might have grasped a stray cat, and yanked her into the well-lit entrance hall. He studied her with daunting sternness.

What he saw was an almost painfully thin girl who looked much younger than her sixteen years. Her threadbare clothing was soaked; her short, tangled hair was so wet that only a hint of its normal vibrant red color was apparent; and her small face—all angles and seemingly filled with huge eyes—was white and pinched. She was no more attractive than a stray mongrel pup.

"Well?"

The vast poise of sixteen years deserted the girl as he barked the one word in her ear. She gulped. "I—I want to be a wizard," she managed finally, defiantly.

"Why?"

She was soaked to the skin, tired, hungry, and possessed a temper that had more than once gotten her into trouble. Her green eyes snapping, she glared up into his handsome, expressionless face, and her voice lost all its timidity.

"I *will* be a wizard! If you won't teach me, I'll find someone who will. I can summon fire already—a little—and I can *feel* the power inside me. All I need is a teacher, and I'll be great one day—"

He lifted her clear off the floor and shook her briefly, effortlessly, inducing silence with no magic at all. "The first lesson an apprentice must learn," he told her calmly, "is to never—ever—shout at a Master."

Then he casually released her, conjured a bundle of clothing out of thin air, and handed it to her. Then he waved a hand negligently and sent her floating up the dark stairs toward a bathroom.

And so it began.

Seattle, Present

His fingers touched her breasts, stroking soft skin and teasing the hard pink nipples. The swollen weight filled his hands as he lifted and kneaded, and when she moaned and arched her back, he lowered his mouth to her. He stopped thinking.

He felt. He felt his own body, taut and pulsing with desire, the blood hot in his veins. He felt her body, soft and warm and willing. He felt her hand on him, stroking slowly, her touch hungry and assured. Her moans and sighs filled his ears, and the heat of her need rose until her flesh burned. The tension inside him coiled more tightly, making his body ache, until he couldn't stand to wait another moment. He sank his flesh into hers, feeling her legs close strongly about his hips. Expertly, lustfully, she met his thrusts, undulating beneath him, her female body the cradle all men returned to. The heat between them built until it was a fever raging out of control, until his body was gripped by the inescapable, inexorable drive for release and pounded frantically inside her. Then, at last, the heat and tension drained from him in a rush . . .

Serena sat bolt upright in bed, gasping. In shock, she stared across the darkened room for a moment, and then she hurriedly leaned over and turned on the lamp on the nightstand. Blinking in the light, she held her hands up and stared at them, reassuring herself that they were hers, still slender and pale and tipped with neat oval nails.

They were hers. She was here and unchanged. Awake. Aware. Herself again.

She could still feel the alien sensations, still see the powerful bronzed hands against paler, softer skin, and still feel sensations her body was incapable of experiencing simply because she was female, not male—

And then she realized.

"Dear God . . . Richard," she whispered.

She had been inside his mind, somehow, in his head just like before, and he had been with another woman. He had been having sex with another woman. Serena had felt what he felt, from the sensual enjoyment of soft female flesh under his touch to the ultimate draining pleasure of orgasm. *She had felt what he felt.*

She drew her knees up and hugged them, feeling tears burning her eyes and nausea churning in her stomach. Another woman. He had a woman somewhere, and she wasn't new because there had been a sense of familiarity in him, a certain knowledge. He knew this woman. Her skin was familiar, her taste, her desire. His body knew hers.

Even Master wizards, it seemed, had appetites just like other men.

Serena felt a wave of emotions so powerful she could endure them only in silent anguish. Her thoughts were tangled and fierce and raw. Not a monk, no, hardly a monk. In fact, it appeared he was quite a proficient lover, judging by the woman's response to him.

On her nightstand, the lamp's bulb burst with a violent sound, but she neither heard it nor noticed the return of darkness to the room.

So he was just a man after all, damn him, a man who got horny like other men and went to some woman who'd spread her legs for him. And often. His trips "out of town" were more frequent these last years. Oh, horny indeed . . .

Unnoticed by Serena, her television set flickered to life, madly scanned though all the channels, and then died with a sound as apologetic as a muffled cough.

Damn him. What'd he do, keep a mistress? Some pretty, pampered blonde—she had been blond, naturally—with empty hot eyes who wore slinky nightgowns and crotchless panties, and moaned like a bitch in heat? Was there only one? Or had he bedded a succession of women over the years, keeping his reputation here in Seattle all nice and tidy while he satisfied his appetites elsewhere?

Serena heard a little sound, and was dimly shocked to realize it came from her throat. It sounded like that of an animal in pain, some tortured creature hunkered down in the dark as it waited helplessly to find out if it would live or die. She didn't realize that she was rocking gently. She didn't see her alarm clock flash a series of red numbers before going dark, or notice that her stereo system was spitting out tape from a cassette.

Only when the overhead light suddenly exploded was Serena jarred from her misery. With a tremendous effort, she struggled to control herself.

"Concentrate," she whispered. "Concentrate. Find the switch." And, for the first time, perhaps spurred on by her urgent need to control what she felt, she did find it. Her wayward energies stopped swirling all around her and were instantly drawn into some part of her she'd never recognized before, where they were completely and safely contained, held there in waiting without constant effort from her.

Moving stiffly, feeling exhausted, Serena got out of bed and moved cautiously across the room to her closet, trying to avoid the shards of glass sprinkled over the rugs and the polished wood floor. There were extra lightbulbs on the closet shelf, and she took one to replace the one from her nightstand lamp. It was difficult to unscrew the burst bulb, but she managed; she didn't trust herself to flick all the shattered pieces out of existence with her powers, not when she'd come so close to losing control entirely.

When the lamp was burning again, she got a broom and dustpan and cleaned up all the bits of glass. A slow survey of the room revealed what else she had destroyed, and she shivered a little at the evidence of just how dangerous unfocused power could be.

Ironically, she couldn't repair what she had wrecked, not by using the powers that had destroyed. Because she didn't understand the technology of television or radio or even clocks, it simply wasn't possible for her to focus her powers to fix what was broken. It would be like the blind trying to put together by touch alone something they couldn't even recognize enough to define.

To create or control anything, it was first necessary to understand its very elements, its basic structure, and how it functioned. How many times had Merlin told her that? Twenty times? A hundred?

Serena sat down on her bed, still feeling drained. But not numb; that mercy wasn't granted to her. The switch she had found to contain her energies could do nothing to erase the memory of Richard with another woman.

It hurt. She couldn't believe how much it hurt. All these years she had convinced herself that she was the only woman in his life who mattered, and now she knew that wasn't true. He didn't belong only to her. He didn't belong to her at all. He really didn't see her as a woman—or, if he did, she obviously held absolutely no attraction for him.

The pain was worse, knowing that.

Dawn had lightened the windows by the time Serena tried to go back to sleep. But she couldn't. She lay beneath the covers staring up at the ceiling, feeling older than she had ever felt before. There was no limbo now, no sense of being suspended between woman and child; Serena knew she could never again be a child, not even to protect herself.

The question was—how was that going to alter her relationship with Merlin? Could she pretend there was nothing different? No. Could she even bear to look at him without crying out her pain and rage? Probably not. How would he react when she made her feelings plain, with disgust or pity? That was certainly possible. Would her raw emotion drive him even farther away from her? Or was he, even now, planning to banish her from his life completely?

Because he knew. He knew what she had discovered in the dark watches of the night.

Just before her own shock had wrenched her free of his mind, Serena had felt for a split-second *his* shock as he sensed and recognized her presence intruding on that intensely private act.

He knew. He knew she had been there.

It was another part of her pain, the discomfiting guilt and

shame of having been, however unintentionally, a voyeur. She had a memory now that she would never forget, but it was his, not hers. She'd stolen it from him . . . . And of all the things they both had to face when he came home, that one was likely to be the most difficult of all.

The only certainty Serena could find in any of it was the knowledge that nothing would ever be the same again.

SILVER FLAME
by Susan Johnson

On Sale in May

She was driven by love to break every rule . . . . Empress
Jordan had fled to the Montana wilderness to escape a cruel
injustice, only to find herself forced to desperate means to
feed her brothers and sisters. Once she agreed to sell her most
precious possession to the highest bidder, she feared she'd made
a terrible mistake—even as she found herself hoping it was the
tall, dark, chiseled stranger who had taken her dare and claimed
her . . . .

Empress stood before him, unabashed in her nudity, and
raising her emerald eyes the required height to meet his so
far above, she said "What *will* you do with me, Mr. Braddock-
Black?"

"Trey," he ordered, unconscious of his lightly commanding tone.

"What *will* you do with me, Trey?" she repeated correcting
herself as ordered. But there was more than a hint of impudence in her tone and in her tilted mouth and arched brow.

Responding to the impudence with some of his own, he
replied with a small smile, "Whatever you prefer, Empress,
darling." He towered over her, clothed and booted, as dark
as Lucifer, and she was intensely aware of his power and size,
as if his presence seemed to invade her. "You set the pace,
sweetheart," he said encouragingly, reaching out to slide the

pad of one finger slowly across her shoulder. "But take your time," he went on, recognizing his own excitement, running his warm palm up her neck and cupping the back of her head lightly. Trey's voice had dropped half an octave. "We've three weeks. . . ." And for the first time in his life he looked forward to three undiluted weeks of one woman's company. It was like scenting one's mate, primordial and reflexive, and while his intellect ignored the peremptory, inexplicable compulsion, his body and blood and dragooned sensory receptors willingly complied to the urgency.

Bending his head low, his lips touched hers lightly, brushing twice across them like silken warmth before he gently slid over her mouth with his tongue and sent a shocking trail of fire curling deep down inside her.

She drew back in an unconscious response, but he'd felt the heated flame, too, and from the startled look in his eyes she knew the spark had touched them both. Trey's breathing quickened, his hand tightened abruptly on the back of her head, pulling her closer with insistence, with authority, while his other hand slid down her back until it rested warmly at the base of her spine. And when his mouth covered hers a second time, intense suddenly, more demanding, she could feel him rising hard against her. She may have been an innocent in the ways of a man and a woman, but Empress knew how animals mated in nature, and for the first time she sensed a soft warmth stirring within herself.

It was at once strange and blissful, and for a brief detached moment she felt very grown, as if a riddle of the universe were suddenly revealed. One doesn't have to love a man to feel the fire, she thought. It was at odds with all her mother had told her. Inexplicably she experienced an overwhelming sense of discovery, as if she alone knew a fundamental principle of humanity. But then her transient musing was abruptly arrested, for under the light pressure of Trey's lips she found hers opening, and the velvety, heated caress of Trey's tongue slowly entered her mouth, exploring languidly, licking her sweetness, and the heady, brandy taste of him was like a fresh treasure to be savored. She tentatively responded like a lambkin to new, unsteady legs, and when her tongue brushed his and did her own unhurried tasting, she heard him groan low in his throat. Swaying gently against her, his hard length pressed more adamantly into her yielding softness. Fire raced downward to a tingling place deep inside her as Trey's strong, insistent arousal throbbed against the soft curve of her stomach. He held her captive with his large hand low on her back as they kissed, and she felt a leaping flame speed along untried nerve endings, creating delicious new sensations. There was strange pleasure in the feel of his soft wool shirt; a melting warmth seeped through her senses, and she swayed closer into the strong male body, as if she knew instinctively that he would rarefy the enchantment. A moment later, as her mouth opened pliantly beneath his, her hands came up of their own accord and, rich with promise, rested lightly on his shoulders.

Her artless naîveté was setting his blood dangerously afire. He gave her high marks for subtlety. First the tentative withdrawal, and now the ingenuous response, was more erotic than any flagrant vice of the most skilled lover. And yet it surely must be some kind of drama, effective like the scene downstairs, where she withheld more than she offered in the concealing men's clothes and made every man in the room want to undress her.

Whether artifice, pretext, sham, or entreating supplication, the soft, imploring body melting into his, the small appealing hands warm on his shoulders, made delay suddenly inconvenient. "I think, sweet Empress," he said, his breath warm on her mouth, "*next* time you can set the pace. . . ."

Bending quickly, he lifted her into his arms and carried her to the bed. Laying her down on the rose velvet coverlet, he stood briefly and looked at her. Wanton as a Circe nymph, she looked back at him, her glance direct into his heated gaze, and she saw the smoldering, iridescent desire in his eyes. She was golden pearl juxtaposed to blush velvet, and when she slowly lifted her arms to him, he, no longer in control of himself, not detached or casual or playful as he usually was making love, took a deep breath, swiftly moved the half step to the bed, and lowered his body over hers, reaching for the buttons on his trousers with trembling fingers. His boots crushed the fine velvet but he didn't notice; she whimpered slightly when his heavy gold belt buckle pressed into her silken skin, but he kissed her in apology, intent on burying himself in the devastating Miss Jordan's lushly carnal body. His wool-clad legs pushed her pale thighs apart, and all he could think of was the feel of her closing around him. He surged forward, and she cried out softly. Maddened with desire, he thrust forward again. This time he *heard* her cry. "Oh, Christ," he breathed, urgent need suffocating in his lungs, "you can't be a virgin." He never bothered with virgins. It had been years since he'd slept with one. Lord, he was hard.

"It doesn't matter," she replied quickly, tense beneath him.

"It doesn't matter," he repeated softly, blood drumming in his temples and in his fingertips and in the soles of his feet inside the custom-made boots, and most of all in his rigid erection, insistent like a battering ram a hair's breadth from where he wanted to be so badly, he could taste the blood in his mouth. It doesn't matter, his conscience repeated. She said it doesn't matter, so it doesn't matter, and he drove in again.

Her muffled cry exploded across his lips as his mouth lowered to kiss her.

"Oh, hell." He exhaled deeply, drawing back, and, poised on his elbows, looked down at her uncertainly, his long dark hair framing his face like black silk.

"I won't cry out again," she whispered, her voice more certain than the poignant depths of her shadowy eyes. "Please . . . I must have the money."

It was all too odd and too sudden and too out of character for him. Damn . . . plundering a virgin, making her cry in fear and pain. *Steady, you'll live if you don't have her,* he told himself, but quivering need played devil's advocate to that platitude. She was urging him on. His body was even more fiercely demanding he take her. "Hell and damnation," he muttered disgruntedly. The problem was terrible, demanding immediate answers, and he wasn't thinking too clearly, only feeling a delirious excitement quite detached from moral judgment. And adamant. "Bloody hell," he breathed, and in that moment, rational thought gained a fingertip control on the ragged edges of his lust. "Keep the money. I don't want to—" He said it quickly, before he'd change his mind, then paused and smiled. "Obviously that's not entirely true, but I don't ruin virgins," he said levelly.

Empress had not survived the death of her parents and the months following, struggling to stay alive in the wilderness, without discovering in herself immense strength. She summoned it now, shakily but determinedly. "It's not a moral dilemma. It's a business matter and my responsibility. I insist."

He laughed, his smile close and deliciously warm. "Here I'm refusing a woman insisting I take her virginity. I must be crazy."

"The world's crazy sometimes, I think," she replied softly, aware of the complex reasons prompting her conduct.

"Tonight, at least," he murmured, "it's more off track than usual." But even for a wild young man notorious as a womanizer, the offered innocence was too strangely bizarre. And maybe too businesslike for a man who found pleasure and delight in the act. It was not flattering to be a surrogate for a business matter. "Look," he said with an obvious effort, "thanks but no thanks. I'm not interested. But keep the money. I admire your courage." And rolling off her, he lay on his back and shouted, *"Flo!"*

"No!" Empress cried, and was on top of him before he drew his next breath, terrified he'd change his mind about the money, terrified he'd change his mind in the morning when his head was clear and he woke up in Flo's arms. Fifty thousand dollars was a huge sum of money to give away on a whim, or to lose to some misplaced moral scruple. She must convince him to stay with her, then at least she could earn the money. Or at least try.

Lying like silken enchantment on his lean, muscled body, she covered his face with kisses. Breathless, rushing kisses, a young girls's simple closemouthed kisses. Then, in a flush of boldness, driven by necessity, a tentative dancing lick of her small tongue slid down his straight nose, to his waiting mouth. When her tongue lightly caressed the arched curve of his upper lip, his hands came up and closed on her naked shoulders, and he drew the teasing tip into his mouth. He sucked on it gently, slowly, as if he envisioned a lifetime without interruptions, until the small, sun-kissed shoulders beneath his hands trembled in tiny quivers.

Strange, fluttering wing beats sped through her heating blood, and a curious languor caused Empress to twine her arms around Trey's strong neck. But her heart was beating hard like the Indian drums whose sound carried far up to their hidden valley in summer, for fear outweighed languor still. He mustn't go to Flo. Slipping her fingers through the black luster of his long hair, ruffled in loose waves on his neck, she brushed her mouth along his cheek. "Please," she whispered near his ear, visions of her hope to save her family dashed by his reluctance, "stay with me." It was a simple plea, simply put. It was perhaps her last chance. Her lips traced the perfect curve of his ears, and his hands tightened their grip in response. "Say it's all right. Say I can stay. . . ." She was murmuring rapidly in a flurry of words.

How should he answer the half-shy, quicksilver words? Why was she insisting? Why did the flattery of a woman wanting him matter?

Then she shifted a little so her leg slid between his, a sensual, instinctive movement, and the smooth velvet of his masculinity rose against her thigh. It was warm, it was hot, and like a child might explore a new sensation, she moved her leg lazily up its length.

Trey's mouth went dry, and he couldn't convince himself that refusal was important any longer. He groaned, thinking, there are some things in life without answers. His hand was trembling when he drew her mouth back to his.

A moment later, when Flo knocked and called out his name, Empress shouted, "Go away!" And when Flo repeated his name, Trey's voice carried clearly through the closed door. "I'll be down later."

He was rigid but tense and undecided, and Empress counted on the little she knew about masculine desire to accomplish what her logical explanation hadn't. Being French, she was well aware that *amour* could be heated and fraught with urgent emotion, but she was unsure exactly about the degree of urgency relative to desire.

But she knew what had happened moments before when she'd tasted his mouth and recalled how he'd responded to her yielding softness, so she practiced her limited expertise with a determined persistence. She must be sure she had the money. And if it would assure her family their future, her virginity was paltry stuff in the bargain.

"Now let's begin again," she whispered.

THE MAGNIFICENT ROGUE
by Iris Johansen

On Sale in August

From the glittering court of Queen Elizabeth to the barren island of Craighdu, THE MAGNIFICENT ROGUE is the spellbinding story of courageous love and unspeakable evil. The daring chieftain of a Scottish clan, Robert MacDarren knows no fear, and only the threat to a kinsman's life makes him bow to Queen Elizabeth's order that he wed Kathryn Ann Kentrye. He's aware of the dangerous secret in Kate's past, a secret that could destroy a great empire, but he doesn't expect the stirring of desire when he first lays eyes on the fragile beauty. Grateful to escape the tyranny of her guardian, Kate accepts the mesmerizing stranger as her husband. But even as they discover a passion greater than either has known, enemies are weaving their poisonous web around them, and soon Robert and Kate must risk their very lives to defy the ultimate treachery.

In the following scene, Robert and his cousin Gavin Gordon have come to Kate's home to claim her—and she flees.

She was being followed!

Sebastian?

Kate paused a moment on the trail and caught a glimpse of dark hair and the shimmer of the gold necklace about her pursuer's neck. Not Sebastian. Robert MacDarren.

The wild surge of disappointment she felt at the realization was completely unreasonable. He must have come at Sebastian's bidding, which meant her guardian had persuaded him to his way of thinking. Well, what had she expected? He was a stranger and Sebastian was a respected man of the cloth. There was no reason why he would be different from any of the others. How clever of Sebastian to send someone younger and stronger than himself to search her out, she thought bitterly.

She turned and began to run, her shoes sinking into the mud with every step. She glanced over her shoulder.

He was closer. He was not running, but his long legs covered the ground steadily, effortlessly, as his gaze studied the trail in front of him. He had evidently not seen her yet and was only following her tracks.

She was growing weaker. Her head felt peculiarly light and her breath was coming in painful gasps. She couldn't keep running.

And she couldn't surrender.

Which left only one solution to her dilemma. She sprinted several yards ahead and then darted into the underbrush at the side of the trail.

Hurry. She had to hurry. Her gaze frantically searched the underbrush. Ah, there was one.

She pounced on a heavy branch and then backtracked several yards and held it, waiting.

She must aim for the head. She had the strength for only one blow and it must drop him.

Her breath sounded heavily and terribly loud. She had to breathe more evenly or he would hear her.

He was almost upon her.

Her hands tightened on the branch.

He went past her, his expression intent as he studied the tracks.

She drew a deep breath, stepped out on the trail behind him, and swung the branch with all her strength.

He grunted in pain and then slowly crumpled to the ground.

She dropped the branch and ran past his body and darted down the trail again.

Something struck the back of her knees. She was falling!

She hit the ground so hard, the breath left her body. Blackness swirled around her.

When the darkness cleared, she realized she was on her back, her arms pinned on each side of her head. Robert MacDarren was astride her body.

She started to struggle.

"Lie still, dammit." His hands tightened cruelly on her arms. "I'm not—Ouch!"

She had turned her head and sunk her teeth into his wrist. She could taste the coppery flavor of blood in her mouth, but his grip didn't ease.

"Let me go!" How stupidly futile the words were when she knew he had no intention of releasing her.

She tried to butt her head against his chest, but she couldn't reach him.

"Really, Robert, can't you wait until the words are said for you to climb on top of her?" Gavin Gordon said from behind MacDarren.

"It's about time you got here," MacDarren said in a growl. "She's trying to kill me."

'Aye, for someone who couldn't lift her head, she's doing quite well. I saw her strike the blow." Gavin grinned. "But I was too far away to come to your rescue. Did she do any damage?"

"I'm going to have one hell of a headache."

Kate tried to knee him in the groin, but he quickly moved upward on her body.

"Your hand's bleeding," Gavin observed.

"She's taken a piece out of me. I can see why Landfield kept the ropes on her."

The ropes. Despair tore through her as she realized how completely Sebastian had won him to his way of thinking. The man would bind her and take her back to Sebastian. She couldn't fight against both MacDarren and Gordon and would use the last of her precious strength trying to do so. She would have to wait for a better opportunity to present itself. She stopped fighting and lay there staring defiantly at him.

"Very sensible," MacDarren said grimly. "I'm not in a very good temper at the moment. I don't think you want to make it worse."

"Get off me."

"And have you run away again?" MacDarren shook his head. "You've caused me enough trouble for one day. Give me your belt, Gavin."

Gavin took off his wide leather belt and handed it to MacDarren, who buckled the belt about her wrists and drew it tight.

"I'm not going back to the cottage," she said with the fierceness born of desperation. "I *can't* go back there."

He got off her and rose to his feet. "You'll go where I tell you to go, even if I have to drag—" He stopped in self-disgust as he realized what he had said. "Christ, I sound like that bastard." The anger suddenly left him as he looked at her lying there before him. "You're afraid of him?"

Fear was always with her when she thought of Sebastian, but she would not admit it. She sat up and repeated, "I can't go back."

He studied her for a moment. "All right, we won't go back. You'll never have to see him again."

She stared at him in disbelief.

He turned to Gavin. "We'll stay the night at that inn we passed at the edge of the village. Go back to the cottage and get her belongings and then saddle the horses. We'll meet you at the stable."

Gavin nodded and the next moment disappeared into the underbrush.

MacDarren glanced down at Kate. "I trust you don't object to that arrangement?"

She couldn't comprehend his words. "You're taking me away?"

"If you'd waited, instead of jumping out the window, I would have told you that two hours ago. That's why I came."

Then she thought she understood. "You're taking me to the lady?"

He shook his head. "It appears Her Majesty thinks it's time you wed."

Shock upon shock. "Wed?"

He said impatiently, "You say that as if you don't know what it means. You must have had instructions on the duties of wifehood."

"I know what it means." Slavery and suffocation and cruelty. From what she could judge from Sebastian and Martha's marriage, a wife's lot was little better than her own. True, he did not beat Martha, but the screams she heard from their bedroom while they mated had filled her with sick horror. But she had thought she would never have to worry about that kind of mistreatment. "I can never marry."

"Is that what the good vicar told you?" His lips tightened. "Well, it appears the queen disagrees."

Then it might come to pass. Even Sebastian obeyed the queen. The faintest hope began to spring within her. Even though marriage was only another form of slavery, perhaps the queen had chosen an easier master than Sebastian for her. "Who am I to marry?"

He smiled sardonically. "I have that honor."

Another shock and not a pleasant one. Easy was not a term anyone would use to describe this man. She blurted, "And you're not afraid?"

"Afraid of you? Not if I have someone to guard my back."

That wasn't what she meant, but of course he wouldn't be afraid. She doubted if he feared anything or anyone, and, besides, she wasn't what Sebastian said she was. He had said the words so often, she sometimes found herself believing him, and she was so tired now, she wasn't thinking clearly. The strength was seeping out of her with every passing second. "No, you shouldn't be afraid." She swayed. "Not Lilith . . ."

"More like a muddy gopher," he muttered as he reached out and steadied her. "We have to get to the stable. Can you walk, or shall I carry you?"

"I can walk." She dismissed the outlandish thought of marriage from her mind. She would ponder the implications of this change in her life later. There were more important matters to consider now. "But we have to get Caird."

"Caird? Who the devil is Caird?"

"My horse." She turned and started through the underbrush. "Before we go I have to fetch him. He's not far. . . ."

She could hear the brush shift and whisper as he followed her. "Your horse is in the forest?"

"I was hiding him from Sebastian. He was going to kill him. He wanted me to tell him where he was."

"And that was why he was dragging you?"

She ignored the question. "Sebastian said the forest beasts would devour him. He frightened me." She was staggering with exhaustion, but she couldn't give up now. "It's been such a while since I left him." She rounded a corner of a trail and breathed a sigh of relief as she caught sight of Caird calmly munching grass under the shelter of an oak tree. "No, he's fine."

"You think so?" MacDarren's skeptical gaze raked the piebald stallion from its swayback to its knobby knees. "I see nothing fine about him. How old is he?"

"Almost twenty." She reached the horse and tenderly began to stroke his muzzle. "But he's strong and very good-tempered."

"He won't do," MacDarren said flatly. "We'll have to get rid of him. He'd never get through the Highlands. We'll leave him with the innkeeper and I'll buy you another horse."

"I won't get rid of him," she said fiercely. "I can't just leave him. How would I know if they'd take good care of him? He goes with us."

"And I say he stays."

The words were spoken with such absolute resolution that they sent a jolt of terror through her. They reminded her of Sebastian's edicts, from which there was no appeal. She moistened her lips. "Then I'll have to stay too."

MacDarren's gaze narrowed on her face. "And what if Landfield catches you again?"

She shrugged and leaned her cheek wearily against Caird's muzzle. "He belongs to me," she said simply.

She could feel his gaze on her back and sensed his exasperation. "Oh, for God's sake!" He picked up her saddle from the ground by the tree and threw it on Caird's back. He began to buckle the cinches. "All right, we'll take him."

Joy soared through her. "Truly?"

"I said it, didn't I?" He picked her up and tossed her into the saddle. "We'll use him as a pack horse and I'll get you another mount to ride. Satisfied?"

Satisfied! She smiled brilliantly. "Oh yes. You won't regret it. But you needn't spend your money on another horse. Caird is really very strong. I'm sure he'll be able to—"

"I'm already regretting it." His tone was distinctly edgy as he began to lead the horse through the forest. "Even carrying a light load, I doubt if he'll get through the Highlands."

It was the second time he had mentioned these forbidding Highlands, but she didn't care where they were going as long as they were taking Caird. "But you'll do it? You won't change your mind?"

For an instant his expression softened as he saw the eagerness in her face. "I won't change my mind."

Gavin was already mounted and waiting when they arrived at the stable a short time later. A grin lit his face as he glanced from Kate to the horse and then back again. "Hers?"

Robert nodded. "And the cause of all this turmoil."

"A fitting pair," Gavin murmured. "She has a chance of cleaning up decently, but the horse . . ." He shook his head. "No hope for it, Robert."

"My thought exactly. But we're keeping him anyway."

Gavin's brows lifted. "Oh, are we? Interesting . . ."

Robert swung into the saddle. "Any trouble with the vicar and his wife?"

Kate's hands tensed on the reins.

"Mistress Landfield appeared to be overjoyed to give me the girl's belongings." He nodded at a small bundle tied to the saddle. "And the vicar just glowered at me."

"Perhaps he's given up."

"He won't give up," Kate whispered. "He never gives up."

"Then perhaps we'd better go before we encounter him again," Robert said as he kicked his horse into a trot. "Keep an eye on her, Gavin. She's almost reeling in that saddle."

Sebastian was waiting for them a short distance from the cottage. He stood blocking the middle of the path.

"Get out of the way," Robert said coldly. "I'm not in the mood for this."

"It's your last chance," Sebastian said. "Give her back to me before it's too late."

"Stand aside, Landfield."

"Kathryn." Sebastian turned to her and his voice was pleading. "Do not go. You know you can never wed. You know what will happen."

Robert rode forward and his horse's shoulder forced Sebastian to the side of the trail. He motioned Gavin and Kate to ride ahead. "It's over. She's no longer your responsibility." His voice lowered to soft deadliness. "And if you ever approach her again, I'll make sure I never see you repeat the mistake."

"You'll see me." Landfield's eyes shimmered with tears as his gaze clung to Kate. "I wanted to spare you, Kathryn. I wanted to save you, but God has willed otherwise. You know what has to be done now."

He turned and walked heavily back toward the cottage.

"What did he mean?" Gavin asked as his curious gaze followed Landfield.

She didn't answer as she watched Sebastian stalk away. She realized she was shivering with a sense of impending doom. How foolish. This was what he wanted her to feel, his way of chaining her to him.

"Well?" Robert asked.

"Nothing. He just wanted to make me afraid." She moistened her lips. "He likes me to be afraid of him."

She could see he didn't believe her and thought he would pursue it. Instead he said quietly, "You don't have to fear him any longer. He no longer holds any power over you." He held her gaze with a mesmerizing power. "I'm the only one who does now."

OFFICIAL RULES TO WINNERS CLASSIC SWEEPSTAKES

No Purchase necessary. To enter the sweepstakes follow instructions found elsewhere in this offer. You can also enter the sweepstakes by hand printing your name, address, city, state and zip code on a 3" x 5" piece of paper and mailing it to: Winners Classic Sweepstakes, P.O. Box 785, Gibbstown, NJ 08027. Mail each entry separately. Sweepstakes begins 12/1/91. Entries must be received by 6/1/93. Some presentations of this sweepstakes may feature a deadline for the Early Bird prize. If the offer you receive does, then to be eligible for the Early Bird prize your entry must be received according to the Early Bird date specified. Not responsible for lost, late, damaged, misdirected, illegible or postage due mail. Mechanically reproduced entries are not eligible. All entries become property of the sponsor and will not be returned.

Prize Selection/Validations: Winners will be selected in random drawings on or about 7/30/93, by VENTURA ASSOCIATES, INC., an independent judging organization whose decisions are final. Odds of winning are determined by total number of entries received. Circulation of this sweepstakes is estimated not to exceed 200 million. Entrants need not be present to win. All prizes are guaranteed to be awarded and delivered to winners. Winners will be notified by mail and may be required to complete an affidavit of eligibility and release of liability which must be returned within 14 days of date of notification or alternate winners will be selected. Any guest of a trip winner will also be required to execute a release of liability. Any prize notification letter or any prize returned to a participating sponsor, Bantam Doubleday Dell Publishing Group, Inc., its participating divisions or subsidiaries, or VENTURA ASSOCIATES, INC. as undeliverable will be awarded to an alternate winner. Prizes are not transferable. No multiple prize winners except as may be necessary due to unavailability, in which case a prize of equal or greater value will be awarded. Prizes will be awarded approximately 90 days after the drawing. All taxes, automobile license and registration fees, if applicable, are the sole responsibility of the winners. Entry constitutes permission (except where prohibited) to use winners' names and likenesses for publicity purposes without further or other compensation.

Participation. This sweepstakes is open to residents of the United States and Canada, except for the province of Quebec. This sweepstakes is sponsored by Bantam Doubleday Dell Publishing Group, Inc. (BDD), 666 Fifth Avenue, New York, NY 10103. Versions of this sweepstakes with different graphics will be offered in conjunction with various solicitations or promotions by different subsidiaries and divisions of BDD. Employees and their families of BDD, its division, subsidiaries, advertising agencies, and VENTURA ASSOCIATES, INC., are not eligible.

Canadian residents, in order to win, must first correctly answer a time limited arithmetical skill testing question. Void in Quebec and wherever prohibited or restricted by law. Subject to all federal, state, local and provincial laws and regulations.

Prizes: The following values for prizes are determined by the manufacturers' suggested retail prices or by what these items are currently known to be selling for at the time this offer was published. Approximate retail values include handling and delivery of prizes. Estimated maximum retail value of prizes: 1 Grand Prize ($27,500 if merchandise or $25,000 Cash); 1 First Prize ($3,000); 5 Second Prizes ($400 each); 35 Third Prizes ($100 each); 1,000 Fourth Prizes ($9.00 each); 1 Early Bird Prize ($5,000); Total approximate maximum retail value is $50,000. Winners will have the option of selecting any prize offered at level won. Automobile winner must have a valid driver's license at the time the car is awarded. Trips are subject to space and departure availability. Certain black-out dates may apply. Travel must be completed within one year from the time the prize is awarded. Minors must be accompanied by an adult. Prizes won by minors will be awarded in the name of parent or legal guardian.

For a list of Major Prize Winners (available after 7/30/93): send a self-addressed, stamped envelope entirely separate from your entry to: Winners Classic Sweepstakes Winners, P.O. Box 825, Gibbstown, NJ 08027. Requests must be received by 6/1/93. DO NOT SEND ANY OTHER CORRESPONDENCE TO THIS P.O. BOX.